Lady Jaided's
PARANORMAL PASSIONS

ELISA ADAMS
MARI BYRNE
KATE DOUGLAS
CATHRYN FOX
MICHELLE PILLOW
CRICKET STARR

ELLORA'S CAVE
ROMANTICA PUBLISHING

The Doll
By Cricket Starr
ॐ

A young woman finds a wooden figure that reminds her of a childhood toy, but there is nothing childish about the invisible stranger who visits soon after she brings the doll home. Soon all her sexual desires are met, except the one she wishes the most — that her unseen lover was real.

More Than a Hunch
By Kate Douglas
ॐ

Nita Franklin's dreams have gone from sensual to wildly erotic. It might be the change, but this intrepid reporter is convinced it's something more. When she meets the object of her nightly passion in person, she learns the truth — Martin Hawley, wealthy, sexy San Francisco aristocrat, wants Nita to help him find his kidnapped daughter.

And he's well aware of the sensual dreams. He's having them, too...

Death Reborn
By Mari Byrne
ॐ

He fell in love with her twenty years ago, the first time he almost had to claim her. Now Death, the Grim Reaper, covets the mortal woman for himself...

Dream Stalker
By Elisa Adams

&

Desperate to be free from the nightmares that have been plaguing her since childhood, Alex volunteers for an experimental treatment designed to release people from the dreams that haunt them at night. When the killer in her mind is mistakenly set free into reality she'll do anything she can to destroy it, even if it means working with a man she knows she can't trust, a man who played a part in the killer's release.

Scorched Destiny
By Michelle Pillow

&

Lucienne's family has searched for centuries to liberate the ancient djinn imprisoned beneath the Arabian sands. Once free, the djinni Nadir will be her slave, forced to grant her every wish, her every desire, her every decadent whim. But in order to control him, she must first prove she has enough passion to make her worthy of being his mistress.

Web of Desire
By Cathryn Fox

&

When Ally Shears, a good witch of Belhaven, discovers her old flame Tanner Cage captured in a silky web courtesy of her wicked witch of a cousin, she concocts a plan to make him pay for deserting her a decade ago.

Tanner is a prisoner to her desires and with the help of a table full of sex toys, Ally's ready to try everything she missed out on years ago. Everything…

But when the captive suddenly becomes the captor, Ally finds herself tangled in a web of desire—of her own making.

An Ellora's Cave Romantica Publication

www.ellorascave.com

Lady Jaided's Paranormal Passions

ISBN 9781419956294
ALL RIGHTS RESERVED.
The Doll Copyright © 2003 Cricket Starr
More than a Hunch Copyright © 2002 Kate Douglas
Death Reborn Copyright © 2002 Mari Byrne
Dream Stalker Copyright © 2002 Elisa Adams
Scorched Destiny Copyright © 2005 Michelle Pillow
Web of Desire Copyright © 2006 Cathryn Fox
Edited by Raelene Gorlinsky.
Cover art by Darrel King.

This book printed in the U.S.A. by Jasmine–Jade Enterprises, LLC.

Trade paperback Publication December 2007

LADY JAIDED'S PARANORMAL PASSIONS

ဢ

THE DOLL
Cricket Starr

ဆ

Chapter One
ഇ

Jenny stared at the small wooden figure. The shelf bearing it was high and for a moment she wondered how she'd spotted it at all, partially hidden behind a set of ceramic cherubs she'd never have looked at twice. Still she had noticed it, peeking at her over the horribly cute china heads. Drawn, she reached up and pulled the figure from its perch, examining it closely with growing interest. It was barely twelve inches high, the naked figure of a man with articulated arms and legs. The size and shape were similar to a male fashion doll she'd owned as a child.

Jenny smiled at the recollection. *Charlie.* He'd come with another name, but she'd quickly changed it to one she liked better. The figure really did remind her of Charlie…with a few differences.

Her doll hadn't had corded muscles like the ones carved into this figure's arms and legs, and when she'd stripped his boy-toy clothes off, he'd worn molded underwear instead of boasting an impressive set of male equipment.

Poor Charlie. He would've loved being built like this.

But he'd had one advantage over this wooden man, his face and hair. Jenny still remembered the wavy brown hair, laughing eyes, and toothpaste bright smile of the little man who'd been a stand-in for her future lover, husband, significant whatever.

Instead of eyes, nose or mouth, the face of the figure in her hand was blank, a smooth plane without any features. The empty space gave her a strange feeling as she slid her fingertip across it. Why such detail elsewhere, but no face?

She turned it over, admiring the workmanship. It really was finely made, this little man. The arms bent at the elbows and wrists, the legs at the knees and ankles. Every joint moved smoothly. His feet had tiny toes, and there were finely detailed fingers on his hands.

Even his buttocks were well formed—she couldn't remember the last time she'd seen an ass as nice as this little man's. Of course, it had been a while since she'd seen any man's naked ass, or cock for that matter. Her love life was as empty as the figurine's face and she barely remembered the last time she'd gotten laid.

She peered closely at the wooden man's penis. Too bad it had been carved in a state of relaxation. With a little imagination, she could see it would be just under two inches long when excited, and given the six to one scale…

Ten inches, maybe more? Wow…a fine tool he'd have if he were life-sized. An unusual heat built up between her thighs as she imagined her little man, but not as little, fully engorged and coming toward her.

Was the figure getting warmer?

"Are you interested in the manikin?"

Jenny startled and turned to face the curio shop's owner, an older woman whose faded beauty was offset by the twinkling eyes behind her glasses.

Feigning nonchalance, Jenny replaced the figure onto the shelf. As soon as it was out of her hands she wanted to snatch it back, but she fought the compulsion. "I'm not sure. How much do you want for it?"

The shopkeeper's mouth twitched up into a glimmer of a knowing smile. "Perhaps not so much. Twenty-five dollars?"

For a figurine of that quality? It was piece of art…she'd expected it to cost far more. Still, she didn't need it, and was low in cash.

But her hands craved the feel of the smooth wooden torso again. She had a spot on her mantel in the living room…no, too public, particularly given how detailed the little figure's cock and balls were. Maybe in her bedroom, next to the bed…

At her hesitation, the other woman's smile became more forced. "Perhaps that is too much." She glanced at the figure on the shelf. "The little man has been here for a long time. I think maybe he wants to come home with you. Twenty dollars, then."

Jenny smiled at the whimsical comment. How could a doll have wants? Still, she'd like him to come home with her and twenty dollars wasn't so much. Pulling a bill from her purse, she handed it over. "I'll take it."

The older woman's hands trembled as she carefully wrapped the figure and put it into a bag, her expression grown wistful. "You will enjoy him, I think. Just be careful what you wish for…you might get it."

Jenny laughed. "Been reading up on Chinese curses?"

Eyes twinkling again, the shopkeeper handed the bag over. "Perhaps. Have a nice night."

An odd thing to say, Jenny thought as she left. It was barely noon, wouldn't "have a nice day" have been more appropriate?

* * * * *

It really did look great next to her bed. The polished surface of the figure gleamed in the lamplight, the fine grain of the wood a nice counterpoint to the glossy white of her bedside table. Jenny peered more closely. What kind of wood was it? It had a reddish hue…perhaps maple?

Whatever it was, she loved it. She bent the figure's arms into a supplicant pose, reaching out. Too bad she didn't have another doll. She could give him a girlfriend to hold.

Of course, when she was a little girl, she'd never let her Charlie hold any of the other dolls. Her friends would come over and put Charlie into the bed with a torpedo breasted blonde or brunette, but Jenny had snatched him away once they were gone. Charlie had always slept with her, in her bed.

Eventually she'd outgrown sleeping with him, but she'd kept him nearby, on the desk, on her bedside table, near her so she could talk to him. When she'd outgrown that, he was put in her closet with her other dolls, but she'd never forgotten him.

The day she'd come home from college to find the box gone, its contents sold at a garage sale, she was desolate.

Now Jenny sighed. When she'd slept with Charlie, she'd imagined that one day it would be a real man she'd have in her bed. Her dream man would be someone she could talk to as she had Charlie, someone to be with.

She'd had her share of lovers, men interested in a good time. She'd had companionship…just no one like the man she'd imagined Charlie would be.

Lately she hadn't even had that.

Jenny lay back on the bed, resting her head on the pillow. It had been a long time since she'd screwed a man, but she'd barely even noticed. The bookstore she'd opened with her friend Cory had become her focus and she'd spent all her energy on it. Today was the first time she'd taken a day off in months and she'd spent it wandering the small shops near her home, including the curio shop she'd visited this morning.

She yawned, exertion from the day catching up with her. Maybe she'd take a nap before making dinner. Reaching over to turn off the lamp, she glanced at the figure standing next to it.

Maybe she'd name it Charlie after her lost doll. Grinning at the whimsy, she settled back into the pillow. It was a good thing she'd bought the figure. She'd barely spent anything on herself in so long and she deserved a little treat.

* * * * *

A soft noise woke her, the sound of something sliding along the comforter next to her. The bed dipped down, not a lot, just a little. In the dark silence of the room she thought she heard a soft exhalation.

Was someone there with her? Something brushed against her shoulder, a phantom fingertip.

"Who's there?" Her voice sounded shaky in her ears.

Heated air touched her as if someone breathed on her cheek. Her heart went into overdrive, the beat speeding into a super-sonic blur.

She heard a voice—gentle, soothing, and somehow familiar, a voice with dark tones that left shivers running down her spine. "Don't be afraid, lovely one. I won't hurt you."

Hot breath blew on her face again, and something touched her mouth, a ghostly finger running along its edge. "My purpose is pleasure, always."

"Who are you?" she whispered, fear still intense but now a new feeling rising in her at this gentle caressing of her lips. "What do you want?"

"I am whatever you want me to be, whatever you want to love."

"Why can't I see you?" Fear edged her words.

Something that might have been a chuckle came from the empty air beside her. "I exist as I am, lovely one...without form until desire steps in, and even then what I can manifest is limited. What you see I can't control but what you wish for I can provide, just as long as your pleasure is ensured."

"My pleasure?"

"As I said, that is my goal. It is perhaps too soon for that, but in the meantime..." His voice trailed off suggestively.

Jenny took the bait. "In the meantime, what?"

Another chuckle. "In the meantime, this."

Phantom lips replaced the phantom finger and captured hers in a lingering embrace. Warm, and damp, and soft, the pressure mounted against her mouth in flickering waves. If she closed her eyes she could swear someone was kissing her, someone who knew how to do it with exceptional skill. Without sight she could swear there was a man lying next to her on the bed, kissing her.

She kept her eyes closed. He continued to kiss her.

Her mouth opened and he furthered his gentle assault. His tongue tangled with hers in a sinuous dance. She noted his taste, the warmth of his mouth and strength of his tongue. He pulled the tip of her tongue into his mouth, sucking on it, and her nipples tightened in reaction.

Raising one hand, she discovered that the lips were attached to a firm chin and soft cheeks without a hint of beard. *There should be some...*On the next pass, her fingers caught against the stubble of a five-o'clock shadow. Excited by this discovery, she explored his features, her fingers moving across the planes of his face.

Abruptly he pulled away and her fingers felt nothing anymore. Opening her eyes confirmed the evidence of her other senses. Whoever—whatever—had been here was now gone.

Disappointment filling her, Jenny glanced at the lighted dial of her clock. It was after eight, she'd slept for nearly two hours. Turning on the lights, she sat up and peered around the empty room. No one was here. She got up, checked the locked window, and confirmed the door to the bedroom was closed. No one was here. No one could have been here, or left without her knowing.

But someone had. Someone had kissed her.

She ran her fingers over her lips, thought she still detected a little of the moisture from his tongue. She licked them and his taste still lingered.

Or did it?

Jenny snorted and shook her head. No one had been here, no one had kissed her. She'd fallen asleep and had a dream, that's all. After getting all worked up over her new doll, and the fact that she'd not been with anyone in far too long, she'd fallen asleep and dreamed up a man.

It had been a dream, just a dream.

Then why did her lips still tingle?

Sitting on the bed, she looked over at her figurine, blank face and dark wood in the lamplight. "You aren't going to be good for me if you make me dream of men that kiss like that. It'll spoil me for other guys."

Hands on his hips, the little figure made no reply.

Still shaking her head, Jenny dragged herself to her feet and headed for the door. Her stomach was growling and she needed to eat. She reached the door before she realized what was wrong. Jenny turned and faced the manikin.

Hadn't she left his arms outstretched?

* * * * *

"Cory, I don't care how tall he is. I'm tired and want to veg out."

"But he's gorgeous. Why would you rather stay home on a Saturday night than go out with a handsome hunk? You need a man, Jenny!"

Cory's voice got louder and Jenny pulled the phone away to protect her ear. She sighed. Cory was her best friend as well as business partner, but that didn't make her right. Jenny didn't need anyone.

"Listen, I want to stay home. There's a great old movie on and I want to curl up on the couch and watch it."

"Marcos likes movies," Cory said slyly. "Maybe he could come over and watch with you?"

"I don't want to entertain tonight. All I want is to slip into my nightgown and get comfy."

"I doubt Marcos would mind a nightgown…so long as he got to take it off."

"Cory, I have no interest in Marcos, or any other man for that matter."

A soft cluck of disapproval came through the phone. "Honey, you need someone, you just don't know it yet. But if you want to let life pass you by, that's your business."

"Life isn't going to pass me by just because I stay home on a Saturday night. Listen, I'll talk to you later, the show is going to start any minute."

It was actually a half hour until the movie's beginning, but Jenny didn't need to spend any more time on the phone arguing. Cory always thought she knew best about everything.

After changing into her nightgown, Jenny spotted the little figure by the bed. Feeling whimsical, she took it with her. "I don't need a man around, I got you to keep me company, Charlie. Let's go watch the movie."

She turned off the lamp next to the couch before settling in, leaving the soft glow of the TV as the only light in the room. It had been a long day and Jenny was as tired as she'd claimed. As good as the film was, her eyes soon grew heavy and she nodded off, Charlie sitting beside her on the couch.

* * * * *

The TV was now a quiet glow in the corner, programming ended for the day. In the dim light, the room was all shadows, dark anticipatory peace.

Gentle hands caressed Jenny's feet and ankles, teasing her toes before moving up to stroke the soft skin at the back of her knees. Shifting on the couch, she was barely aware of her nightgown gliding up her legs, baring her thighs, or the pressure of hands urging her knees apart. Her underwear slid off in one fluid movement, not disturbing her peace at all.

What she did notice was a delicious stroking of the tender skin that led to her folds, followed by a warm puff of air.

She spread her legs farther in response.

When the delicate tip of a tongue flicked across her clit, she nearly rose off the couch. Only the presence of strong hands holding her tight against the cushions kept her in place, ready for the next tender assault, which followed immediately. In moments Jenny was writhing about, the sensation of a warm moist mouth on her clit and cunt driving her wild.

Had she really said she didn't need a man? That idle thought drove through her, chased immediately by the comprehension that she most definitely needed this!

In fact, she needed far more of this than she could ever remember needing!

A low moan drove through her throat and her hands reached to feel her lover's head, whose lips massaged her nether parts with such skill. Under her hands she felt a smooth surface, round and hard. She explored it, felt nothing to distinguish any part of it.

It was like she was being given head by a volleyball. Disturbed, she tried to pull away, only to have her hands grabbed by stronger ones. The lips left her crotch, aching and wet.

A quiet voice sounded in her ears. "You're frightened— don't be."

"What are you...you aren't real," she whispered, desperation in her voice.

"I am as real as you wish me to be. Think of what I could be."

In her mind came an image, of a head of hair, brown, thick, and wavy, long enough to twist around her fingers, long enough to clutch in passion.

A deep male chuckle greeted her thought and her hands were pulled back to where they'd been before. Again she felt the roundness of a man's skull, but now it was covered with silky hair that rippled under her fingers.

"Anything you want me to be, I will be, lovely one. Now, hold on as I take you to paradise."

Again his lips descended on her clit and sucked another moan out of her. In moments she was writhing again, this time her hands anchored in soft hair. His hands moved to her buttocks, lifting them, giving him better access, fingers digging in and massaging the round cheeks.

Alternating, sucking hard on her clit, then thrusting his tongue deep into her cunt, her unseen lover drove her to distraction, into a place she barely recognized. It had been a long time since she'd had a man's mouth between her legs. Jenny moaned, then whimpered as the sensation grew more intense, waves of pre-orgasmic fire slipping along the nerves in her arms, her legs, settling into a fireball just below her belly.

One finger explored the crack along her backside, lingering on the tiny puckered opening there, teasing the muscle with sly intent. He sucked long and hard on her clit, and her anus blossomed open under his finger's probing.

Wow, she hadn't expected that! As his finger entered her, the fireball in her belly exploded into raging flame that scattered along her limbs. Jenny quivered as he probed and sucked her, allowing the sensation of his touch to overload her senses. She'd never felt anything to match his mouth, or his wayward finger.

Orgasmic waves flooded her, drowning her shriek of pleasure, and Jenny lost awareness of anything for what felt like forever. Paradise surrounded her, fluffy blue clouds in a white sky echoed in her mind, her body aching in relief from the erotic tension she'd accumulated.

The clouds and sky faded to dark, the dark of her living room, the still dimly lit TV in the corner casting a faint glow. In the shadowed room, the sound of her labored breathing was loud, her heartbeat still raced under the nightgown wadded around her waist.

What the hell? Her lover had disappeared again, the existence of his hands, mouth, and tongue gone with her fading orgasm. Reaching between her legs, Jenny felt her slit, wet and throbbing from where he'd been.

Even her anus still tingled.

She sat up, pulled her wayward gown back into position, and turned on the lamp, letting the light drive the last of the erotic shadows from the room. Trembling, she tried to make sense of what had happened. Someone had been here…someone had made her come with his mouth.

She'd felt his hair.

Examining her fingers, she found a single strand wrapped around her pinkie, thick, wavy, and brown. Trembling, she pulled it and let it fall on the table under the light, to lie next to her missing panties.

This was getting pretty weird.

Getting up, she found Charlie had fallen into the crack of the cushions. Rescuing him, she glared into his featureless face. The smoothness of his head reminded her of what she'd first felt with her hands, the volleyball.

"Charlie, do you know what's going on?"

She was almost surprised when he didn't answer her.

Chapter Two

ഔ

"Is it possible to have an erotic dream that feels so real you have an orgasm?"

Cory laughed as she put away the last of the best-seller list into its slot, her black eyes dancing with merriment. "Honey, you having dreams about sex? You need to get you some real loving, that'll make you sleep well."

For once Jenny didn't argue with her partner, although she found it hard to believe that anything could have been better than last night's adventure. Exhausted after the session on the couch, she'd crawled off to bed and slept without interruption, to discover in the morning that in her haste to reach her bedroom, she'd left Charlie on the couch.

For a moment, quickly dismissed, she wondered if that's why she'd slept so well.

She turned to face her friend, who was still chuckling. "I was just wondering, Cory."

"Oh, I know, honey. And you're entitled to whatever dreams you have. Sure, erotic dreams can make you come, particularly if you're dreaming about someone hot." The woman tossed her red hair out of her face like a teenager rather than the thirty-six Jenny knew her to be. She wiggled her fingers playfully. "So, who's the lucky man?"

Well, he was shaped like a volleyball, but with brown hair and the most talented tongue ever known. Oh, yeah, and invisible…

"I wasn't dreaming about anyone in particular."

"Really?" Cory's smirk said she didn't believe her. "Anyway, I have to dust the back shelves."

Jenny watched the woman waltz down the aisle singing, "Once Upon a Dream" from Sleeping Beauty, the off-key notes lilting through the rows of bookshelves.

She grinned. *If only you knew, Cory.*

* * * * *

It was Jenny's turn to mind the store that evening, so it was late when she got home. The sight of Charlie, one arm raised in a salute, made her smile as she entered her bedroom and headed for the bath. After a long hot day, a shower sounded good.

Wanting company, she plucked the wooden man from his spot by the bed and gave him a perch on the countertop in the bathroom as she stripped. When she realized she was putting on a show for the doll, slowly removing her top and bra to reveal her breasts one by one, she laughed and pulled the rest of her clothes off without further fanfare. What silliness to try and impress a wooden man!

Stepping into the shower felt like heaven, and she luxuriated under the spray for countless moments before reaching for the soap. Eyes closed, she leaned back to wet her hair…only to bump into a solid mass behind her.

Shocked, Jenny tried to turn, but strong arms encircled her, holding her in place. A familiar voice whispered into her ear. "Why did you stop, lovely one? I enjoyed watching you take off your clothes."

Her knees turned to jelly and she might have fallen if he hadn't held her tight. Opening her eyes, she stared down at the spot where she felt his arms cross her chest. Her breasts were flattened, and there was a peculiar vacancy in space before them, a place where the steam from the shower wasn't.

She was being held by an invisible man. "What do you want?" she asked, her voice trembling.

"The same as before. To pleasure you. Have I not pleasured you already?" His voice was a sultry purr in her ears.

"Yes, but…what are you…who are you?"

She actually felt the sigh that passed through his chest behind her. "You ask so many questions, lovely one. I am what I am, what you make of me." Hot breath whispered across the back of her neck and she realized she couldn't feel the spray of the shower, that his body, while unseen, was blocking the water.

She couldn't feel the water but she could feel something else, hard and close to ten inches long, prodding her back. He pulled her closer and rubbed the head of his cock along her spine, letting it linger in the crevice of her behind.

Jenny's mouth went dry. This was not a dream—not wide awake and in the shower. She should say something, make him stop, make him go away…

His hand dipped between her legs and invisible fingers teased her clit, which throbbed into happy awareness. "Are you sure I can't do something for you?"

Jenny couldn't help it. Moaning, she spread her legs and gave him access. Her mysterious lover didn't need any further invitation, and soon had her on her toes, his busy fingers driving her to distraction, milking her clit and delving deep within her pussy. His other hand found occupation with her nipples, tweaking them and rolling them between fingers and thumb. At first she watched, but the sight of her breasts being kneaded by an unseen hand was too strange. It was easier to relax when she kept her eyes closed.

"You are so responsive, my lovely. I love to touch you."

"When can I touch you?"

He chuckled, but there was a sad note to it. "It doesn't quite work that way. But you will feel me, as much of me as I can give you." His cock continued to poke suggestively at her backside, sending her thoughts to intimate activities she'd read about but never experienced.

Another masculine laugh resulted.

She was urged forward to put her hands on the side of the shower wall. "Hand me the soap," he whispered.

Unsure of his intentions, she did, holding it over her shoulder, and felt the bar slip through her fingers. It traveled down her back in a circular motion that felt marvelous. *This man could wash her back anytime.*

But he didn't stay on her back, and soon she felt the soap in a much more intimate place. Trying to turn, she found herself fixed in place, a strong arm holding her as one soapy finger broached a part of her never visited by man before.

"You aren't going to…" Her voice startled when a second finger joined the first, stretching her anus open. The action should have been disconcerting, but somehow it wasn't. Unconsciously her ass tipped higher, making it easer for him to tease the opening further, and she moaned as a third finger joined the two already inside her. Her heartbeat pounded in her ears and she barely heard his next words over it.

"Lovely one, I'm going to give you a new experience, do something you've never done before. You've thought about it at times…but never dared asked. Do you trust me?"

Did she? She wasn't even sure who or what he was. "I don't know…"

Something much larger than a finger pressed into her now relaxed and well-lubricated anus. He entered slowly, giving her ample time to grow used to the invasion. It was startling but not painful, and as he inched inside, her apprehensions slipped into appreciation.

"Oh, well…that is different," she managed to get out between moans.

From behind came a groan at her approval, and he pushed himself deeper, then pulled out with equal deliberation. He repeated the action, first slowly, then faster.

As he sped up, the movement pushed her into the wall, the cool tile almost a relief from the heat of the unseen body behind her. His cock filled her from behind while invisible fingers teased her clit to the point of release.

Jenny moaned and clutched at the arm around her waist, too overcome to realize she was digging her fingers into empty air. How could she have lived this long without experiencing this?

Along the side of her face, she felt the stubble of his beard, his breath hard in her ears. He deepened his stroke and she felt his balls strike her ass in rhythm. "Scream for me. Give me the evidence of your pleasure."

Orgasm seized her and Jenny cried out, her voice echoing off the shower walls. Her body pulsed and shook as her mind gave in to the need to not think, not reason, but simply feel, and what she felt was wonderful. Only as she came back to herself did she realize that while she'd climaxed, he hadn't. His breathing was still hard with passion, the body behind her stiff with unresolved need.

Even so, as the ripples of her passion faded, she felt him fade too, the hold of his arm weakening, the cock inside her slipping away into nothing. Cooling water from the shower rained against her back.

A final warm breath touched her cheek, the light touch of invisible lips on her neck. "Who are you?" she asked, her voice a thready whisper, still in the thrall of the most shattering orgasm she'd ever experienced.

She felt his hesitation, then, with even his voice fading away, she heard him answer.

"Jenny, you can call me Charlie."

* * * * *

Wrapped in a towel, Jenny stared at the little wooden doll sitting next to the sink. It was a good thing the face on it was blank. She'd hate it if it had a smug, self-satisfied smile.

"You're a doll. You are only a doll, made of wood, that's all you are. You can't come to life as an invisible man, you can't be making love to me!"

The figure had no answer.

* * * * *

Maybe she should throw it away. Or burn it. Ideas flooded into her mind, only to be discarded as soon as they got there. She had no proof it was the doll. Maybe she was going crazy. Maybe the doll was a possessed toy — possessed by a demon!

Maybe it was the reincarnation of her old doll Charlie. Could dolls be reincarnated?

Jenny shook her head to clear out the remaining useless ideas, and leaned back on the couch, staring at the wooden figure on the coffee table. Her fireplace was just for show and the stove was electric. She wasn't going to burn it in a trashcan and set off the building's smoke detector.

There was no reason to believe that throwing it away would help. She wouldn't be surprised if Charlie would come back from the trash, covered in eggshells and coffee grounds, and holding a grudge against her. She'd seen enough horror movies.

Besides, he hadn't really hurt her. He'd scared her, but he'd also given her the best sex of her life, and what they'd done in the shower had always been a secret fantasy of hers. Fulfilling her dreams was scarcely something to punish him for.

Jenny groaned. Him…she was thinking of it as a "him".

Well, he was certainly male…that was one thing she could state unequivocally, she thought, rubbing her ass. She still couldn't believe she'd allowed that.

She still couldn't believe she'd enjoyed it, either.

Jenny shook her head again. This was getting her nowhere. What was she going to do? She needed to talk to Charlie and find out what was happening. Why had he come to life and made love to her? To talk to him, she needed to get him here, in a form she could talk to.

An idea sprang into her mind. He'd shown up when she was distracted in the shower, or sleeping on the couch, or in the bedroom, and always when the doll was nearby. When she'd gone to bed last night, she'd left the figure in the living room, and had slept undisturbed.

If she wanted to talk to him, she should keep him with her at all times, particularly in the bedroom at night.

The idea of a nocturnal visitation and all that would entail sent shivers of anticipation down her spine. One thing about it, she was definitely going to have to reconsider her no-men policy. Cory was right that she needed to get out more. Maybe then a wooden doll wouldn't have become the most exciting thing in her life in the past several years.

Snatching up the figure from the coffee table, Jenny strode purposefully to the bedroom. Time to get this started.

Two hours later, she looked up from her book and stared at the figure on the bedside table. Maybe she was wrong. Maybe she was crazy. An invisible man screwing her in the shower and claiming the name of her new toy didn't exactly mean she was sane.

Maybe he was gone, and wouldn't ever return. A wave of sadness passed through her at that thought. She would miss Charlie if that were so.

Placing a bookmark to hold her page, Jenny closed her book and put it on the table. With or without her unseen lover, it was time to go to bed.

Reaching over to turn off the lamp, she glanced at the wooden figure, sitting with knees bent. For a moment she considered taking it to the living room where it had spent the night before.

No, if he wanted to make another appearance tonight, she'd welcome him, but before she let him do anything she'd get some answers!

Switching off the light, she leaned back into the pillows and soon was fast asleep.

* * * * *

Jenny awoke to a solid mass on the bed next to her, a strong arm around her waist, clutching her close. The soft whisper of her name sounded in her ear, "Jenny, wake up."

Startling to full alert, she twisted under the arm and turned to face the emptiness next to her. "Who are you?"

A hand caressed her cheek, and she felt his hot breath in her face. "I told you earlier. You named me Charlie."

"Are you the doll? The manikin?"

The hand on her face moved lower, leaving electric trails along her neck. "That is one manifestation of me. Your skin is so soft...I could touch it for hours."

She ignored his last comment, although his touch was considerably more difficult to dismiss. "Why are you here?"

"To make love to you. To give you pleasure. To grant any wish you have."

That last phrase caught her attention. "My wishes? You do wishes?"

"Only those that I can fulfill. I can give you pleasure. Don't you want pleasure, Jenny?"

His hands had moved to her breasts, her gown falling open as he reached them. *Oh, great, even her clothing was enchanted.* Under his tender care her nipples sprang to full erectness, the surrounding tissue enjoying the massage.

A small moan escaped her and she almost forgot her next question.

Fortunately he repeated his. "Don't you want pleasure?"

Regaining her senses, she caught the invisible hand with her own. "I want pleasure. I want to give it, too."

Again sadness radiated from him as it had in the shower. "I can give you pleasure, Jenny. I want to do that. Taking it...it's hard to explain."

She pulled his hand to her face and kissed it. It felt smooth, like wood. A hand shouldn't feel like wood, it should be soft, have hair...when she pressed it again to her lips, she felt the tickle of tiny hairs along its back and the skin gave under the pressure of her mouth.

"I'm a fairly smart person, Charlie. Try explaining it to me."

His sigh brushed her cheek. "I'm what you've experienced, Jenny, a creature disembodied, unreal. I'm nothing more than a spirit in your world, tied to the doll. But when I'm with someone who needs me, someone who wants me, I can become real...in a sense. You can feel me because it is needed, so I can make love to you."

"You can become solid if I want you to?"

"I'm as solid as I am, as real as I have ever gotten before." He pulled her hand to his head to feel the soft strands slide between her fingers. "I've got hair, Jenny. I've never had that before. You make me more than I ever was."

She ran her fingers down his neck, feeling the ears that had just formed, moved her hand to his chest to feel his heartbeat. Under her fingers it made a ragged tattoo. "If you're so real, why can't I see you?"

Another heartfelt sigh escaped him, and she was sorry she'd asked.

"I can never be that real, Jenny. There are limits to all wishes. The most I can be is a lover for you when you need me to be. Isn't that enough?"

Was it enough? She suppressed her own sigh. It was everything he could offer, so it would have to be.

"Jenny...do you want me to make love to you now?"

She couldn't ignore the plaintive note to his voice. "Yes, Charlie, I do."

Moments later her nightgown was on the floor, Jenny unclear as to how it had gotten there. He lay on top of her—as far as she could tell. When she closed her eyes it was easier to keep track of him, when her vision wasn't arguing with the rest of her senses.

He was kissing her deeply, hungrily, as a starving man would consume a first meal. Lips met and tongues entangled and her desire rose in answer to his. He was her lover, invisible perhaps, but what was the harm in that? She could enjoy him when she needed him. Putting her arms around him, she held him close. When his form shifted and her hold slipped, she wished him more solid. It worked; he stabilized and she hugged him closer.

"Jenny you are a powerful wisher. You have more strength than the others, more control."

His whispered appreciation threw cold water on the flames of her passion. She broke away from his embrace. "Others? What others?"

"I've been a doll for many years. I don't know how to measure the passage of time. I've had other owners…"

"Owners? Like you're a slave?"

"In a sense. I am bound to the doll. I've been like this with other women. Does that matter? Haven't you been with other men?"

Put that way… "Well, yes, I have," she admitted.

A tender hand pushed the hair from her face. "I've been with others, you've been with others. All that matters is that we are together right now. For what it is worth, I love you best."

"Love me?"

"Only when I'm with someone am I alive. You give me life, Jenny. I love you."

In all her years she'd never heard the words from a man. Not that she was hearing them from one now…but it didn't matter.

Jenny placed her hands along his face. "Make love to me, Charlie."

His sensual chuckle answered. "Yes, ma'am."

Hands caressed her breasts and teased her nipples into aching nubs of sensation, an invisible mouth suckling each as her hands were buried in his hair. His mouth left a tingling trail down her belly until it found her core, and licked and tickled her clit and pussy until she was ready to scream.

She tugged on his head until he rose over her again. With her eyes closed she could almost "see" him, feel the tension in his arms as he held his weight above her, hear the ragged breathing from his throat.

Reaching between them, she found his hard-as-wood cock, solid as a chunk of maple. She stroked it and the surface softened, gained the texture of flesh, and pre-cum slicked her palm. Running her fingers along his shaft, the skin moved and revealed the thick knob at the top.

He gasped, letting her work for a short time before his hand fell atop hers. "It doesn't work that way, Jenny. I'm to pleasure you."

"This is pleasure, Charlie. To give pleasure *is* my pleasure."

"But," his voice was strained. "I can't take it."

"If I wish you to, you can. Isn't that right?"

"I suppose…" He didn't sound convinced.

"Let me touch you, Charlie. Please."

She felt him roll off her and settle onto the bed next to her, hesitation rising off him. She found his cock again and ran her hands along it, sensing his muscles stiffen at the sensation. Her hands worked up and down along the shaft, teasing the head with a gentle massage until she heard an appreciative groan erupt from his lips. "Oh, that feels so good, Jenny."

It did feel good. And this was going to feel better. She climbed on top of him, positioning herself to take him, the tip of his cock just outside her pussy.

Once, twice she rubbed it along her cleft, enjoying the feel of him sliding across her clit. On the third pass he seized her hips and embedded himself deep within her. Jenny's cry echoed in the room.

He trembled beneath her. "So wonderful, to be with you."

It was wonderful. And then he moved and it got better. And better. And better still. His cock inside her was warm, hard, even if it was invisible, and sitting astride him she was impaled by its ten-inch length. Each movement was better than the last as invisible hands grasped her waist and guided her up and down along his shaft. Jenny clutched the unseen shoulders under her and hung on as she rode Charlie into another orgasm. Tension and sensation drove each other in her mind and body and she couldn't hold back from the edge any longer. She collapsed with a cry of delight.

Echoes of her climax were still strumming through her when he twisted her to lie beneath him. "Are you ready to do that again?" he whispered.

Without waiting for her answer, he pushed deeper inside over and over, this time filling her even more than before. Jenny reveled in the feel of him, the strength and power of his thrust, driving her deep into the pillows behind her. This was real lovemaking, even if her lover was anything but real.

She arched against him and met the drive of his hips with her own. Heat from his unseen body blasted into her, and the quivers of incipient climax made her pussy clutch at his cock with each withdrawal. Through veils of passion she felt his tension rising to meet hers.

It wasn't enough to take her release. Jenny needed his as well. She clutched his back. "Come with me, Charlie."

"I wish I could," he ground out, the sound harsh as if coming through gritted teeth.

"I wish it too."

Just as she said it, a long shudder passed through the invisible body above her, rippling under her hands. Charlie drove in again, and again, then stopped and tensed. She felt another shudder run through his torso. A low growl came out of him.

He pulled back once more and pushed forward, and this time the growl became a roar, his cock pulsing inside her. Amazed at his reaction, Jenny slipped off the edge again and into the chasm of completion, following Charlie into its depths.

When she returned to herself, still trembling from the experience, Charlie was collapsed on top of her, his pleasant weight reassuring, if deceptively solid.

"Are you all right?" she asked.

His laugh was the shakiest she'd ever heard. "It's been…years since I've done that. Felt that. I'd forgotten…"

"How good it feels?"

He gave another shaky laugh. "Yeah, that."

She felt him start to fade away. "Charlie, don't go."

"I can't stay, Jenny. Much as I want to."

"But you can. I wish you to stay."

His weight was almost gone from her. "It won't work this time. Only during times of strong emotions, of passion, will a wish work. There are limits to everything."

"But Charlie…"

His last breath sounded in her ear. "Goodbye, Jenny. I'll see you tomorrow."

And he was gone.

* * * * *

Jenny lay awake in the stillness of pre-dawn, her mind awhirl with thoughts and emotions. After Charlie's vanishing act last night, sleep had eluded her, and now she faced the dawn with a mixture of wishes, wants, and needs she never realized she had before.

Needs. Cory was right. Jenny hadn't thought she needed anyone, but now that she'd been with Charlie, she knew that was wrong. Physically, mentally, she needed a man far more than she'd expected.

Wants. Charlie had shown her that it was someone like him that she wanted. A man sensitive to her needs as a woman, able to fulfill her fantasies.

Wishes. This was the toughest of all because she knew just what her wish was. She needed and wanted a man just like Charlie. He had touched her in ways she'd never known, had found the passion hidden inside her and brought it to the surface. Charlie was her ultimate fantasy lover.

Unfortunately a fantasy was all he was. She could have him when she needed sex, but not otherwise. He could love her, but only in the most physical way.

She couldn't talk with him, eat with him, or hold him close at night in her bed. He would always be a fantasy, a wonderful one, but never real. He could never be her companion, just a doll with special properties. Very special properties, but those weren't enough, not enough to build a life on.

She needed a man like Charlie, she wanted a man like Charlie, she wished she could have a man like Charlie, but Charlie himself wasn't enough.

Through the windows the sun's light came, a new day dawning. The first day of the rest of her life—yet another cliché, not unlike the one the shopkeeper who'd sold her Charlie had said: "Be careful what you wish for, you might get it."

Jenny pulled herself from her sleepless bed. She'd certainly gotten the wish thing right. She'd wished for Charlie and gotten him. Now what was she going to do with him?

Keeping him with her wasn't a good idea. She needed to get on with her life, find a real man to give her the companionship she needed. So long as Charlie was around it would be awkward. Imagine if he showed up when she had a man over?

Some guys might like that...but she wasn't sure she would.

She could keep him in a drawer or in the closet, and pull him out on special occasions like an elaborate sex toy that didn't need batteries. Jenny looked at the little wooden figure sitting by the bed. Something in his attitude, the air of desolation about it, told her he knew her thoughts.

No, the closet wasn't the answer. He needed to be loved...if not by her, then by someone else. She should take him back to the store and let someone else have him.

Chapter Three
ഇ

The wooden figure was warm in her hands as she handed it to the shopkeeper, whose eyes were sharp and knowing. "He didn't please you?"

Jenny struggled for an answer. "I liked him just fine. But I've decided he didn't fit in well at my apartment."

"Oh?" A twinkle came into the old woman's eyes. "I see. Very well." She reached into her cash drawer and pulled a twenty out. "I'll refund your money, then."

Jenny waved the bill away. "No, that's okay. I don't want it back. I enjoyed having him too much."

"Really?" A smile took over the shopkeeper's face. "In that case, maybe you should say goodbye to him. He likes that." She handed the doll back to Jenny and headed for another part of the store.

Awkwardly, Jenny held the figure and stared at the blank face. "I'm sorry about this, Charlie," she whispered, hoping the shopkeeper wouldn't overhear. "You were terrific, you really were. You taught me a lot about myself, and what I want. But you did too good a job. I need more from a man than a good time once in a while. I need someone who will be there with me, even when we aren't having sex, and that isn't you."

She put the doll on the counter top and stroked its back one last time. "Goodbye, Charlie, and good luck with your next owner. I hope her wishes are strong like mine so you can enjoy yourself."

Her hand lingered on his head, and inexplicably her eyes filled with tears. "I wish you could be the man I want." Under her fingers, a sudden heat flashed, then dispersed.

Tearing her tingling fingers away, she dashed the moisture from her eyes and fled the shop, not caring how strange the owner thought her abrupt exit.

* * * * *

"I'm going for lunch, honey," Cory said, breaking Jenny out of the half-asleep, half-miserable funk she'd been in since opening the store. "Do you want me to bring you back something?"

Jenny attempted a smile. "No, it's okay. I'm not very hungry. I'll get something later."

Cory gave her a troubled look. "Are you okay? You look like you lost your best friend."

In some sense, Charlie had been her best friend. Shaking her head, Jenny managed a real smile. "I'll be fine, Cory. Go get your lunch."

Working through some of the accounting books kept her busy until the store filled with customers on their lunch break. Jenny answered questions and rang up sales for an hour, then the crowd cleared out and she was able to get back to the books.

She smiled in satisfaction at the recorded receipts. They were making a good profit this month.

"Excuse me, I'm looking for a book."

The voice was shockingly familiar and it jerked Jenny's head out of the accounts. She stared up at her customer, a young man whose cheeks sported the hint of a beard and whose brown wavy hair was just long enough to wrap around her fingers. Gray eyes held a hint of laughter in them, and when he smiled his teeth were toothpaste white.

He was smiling now.

Jenny searched for and found her voice. "What kind of book are you looking for?"

The smile turned into a grin. "It's an old classic. A kid's book I believe. About a wooden boy who wanted to become real?"

This was getting stranger by the minute. "Pinocchio? You want the original version or the one from the movie?"

He leaned against the counter. "Oh, I always think the original is best, don't you, lovely one?"

It was too much. *"Charlie?"*

Warmth darkened his eyes. "That's my name."

"But how, why?" she sputtered.

He leaned closer and stopped her inarticulate speech with a lingering kiss. Closing her eyes, Jenny felt again his lips capture hers, warm and damp and soft, and gave herself up to the sheer pleasure of it, a dream come true. By the time the kiss ended, she knew for certain this was her Charlie, come to life.

She gazed into his gray eyes. "I can't believe this."

"I told you that you were a powerful wisher. That last wish at the shop was a doozy."

"So you're real now?"

"As real as you." He ran a finger down her cheek. Then his stomach growled. "And hungry, too."

The bell on the door broke through their reverie and both turned to see Cory standing, elbows out and hands on hips, a look of surprise and delight on her face. "Looks like you found your friend."

Jenny grinned her response. "I think I'll get lunch now, Cory."

Eyebrows forming perfect crescents above her eyes, Cory watched them head for the door, Charlie's arm possessively around Jenny's waist. "Maybe you should take the rest of the afternoon, as well?"

Getting Charlie home and seeing in the flesh what she'd been intimate with sounded like a great way to spend the rest of the day. "Maybe I will."

"Hey, aren't you going to introduce us?"

Jenny halted in her tracks. She smiled up into Charlie's face. "Cory, this is Charlie…" A look of bewilderment took over her face. "Do you have a last name?"

He grinned. "Of course I do, lovely one. It's Woodman."

The End

Also by Cricket Starr

∽

Divine Interventions 1: Violet Among the Roses
Divine Interventions 2: Echo in the Hall
Divine Interventions 3: Nemesis of the Garden
Ellora's Cavemen: Dreams of the Oasis III (*anthology*)
Ellora's Cavemen: Legendary Tails I (*anthology*)
Fangs for the Memories
Ghosts of Christmas Past
Holiday Reflections *with Reese Gabriel*
Memories to Come
Memories Revised
Perfect Hero
Rogues *with Liddy Midnight*
Two Men and a Lady (*anthology*)

About the Author

డ

Cricket Starr lives in the San Francisco Bay area with her husband of more years than she chooses to count. She loves fantasies, particularly sexual fantasies, and sees her writing as an opportunity to test boundaries. Her driving ambition is to have more fun than anyone should or could have. While published in other venues under her own name, she's found a home for her erotica writing here at Ellora's Cave.

Cricket welcomes comments from readers. You can find her website and email address on her author bio page at www.ellorascave.com.

Tell Us What You Think

We appreciate hearing reader opinions about our books. You can email us at Comments@EllorasCave.com.

MORE THAN A HUNCH
Kate Douglas

ဆာ

Chapter One
ᔓ

I am alive to his familiar presence; it is powerful, sensual, compelling. He steps out of the shadows into an indistinct shimmer of light. I must look at him. Turning away is not an option. He exudes power – power laced with enough potent sensuality to bring a flush to my face and throat and a heavy ache to my loins.

He is nude, clothed only in muscle and sinew, a thick mat of iron gray hair defines his chest, trails down his belly where it darkens and shades his groin. I am naked as well, my flesh tingling with expectation – knowledge – my breasts aching with the sense of what might be.

His cock is a rampant beast. It exudes power and strength, but the length and breadth of his erection is not what compels me. Though I see it, acknowledge it, his eyes are what draw me.

Dark, glinting in the pale light, reflecting shards of blue diamond; they're inhuman, compelling. Uneasy, afraid of their power, I study his face, the forceful line of his jaw, the commanding, arrogant tilt of his head. I should know him. Something about him tugs at my memories, begs me to recall – but the need to remember cannot compete. I am lost, floundering deep within his dark, hypnotic gaze.

Suddenly, without sound or warning, the shadows burst into brilliant light, throwing his tall figure into stark relief. I cry out. He reaches for me, reaches out of the light and takes my hand. His touch is magic, elemental, as our fingers touch, brush lightly, grasp and hold.

There is knowledge in his touch, a sensual knowing I have yearned for, prayed for. My breasts ache, my nipples tighten in heady expectation. Thick moisture dampens the sensitive folds between my legs.

I want.

45

I need.

My fingers clasp his ever more tightly. He draws me closer, his mouth hovering barely the space of a breath from my waiting mouth. I lick my lips. I am aware of his dark gaze, his eyes following the damp sweep of my tongue.

He reaches out, his fingers so close, almost touching the swell of my breast.

Suddenly, we're wrenched apart.

I stumble, reach for him again, but I'm falling, falling away from the light, away from the mystifying stranger, falling until the sound of the ocean crashing against the cliffs grows louder in my ears, pounds faster, faster in cadence with my racing heart, my aching breasts, the soft clenching of the muscles between my thighs.

* * * * *

"Damned hot flash!" Fighting the remnants of terror, the frantic heat of sex unfulfilled, I groped for the lamp on the table next to the bed. Perspiration flowed in rivulets between my breasts and my hair clung to my neck and face.

I grabbed my notebook, scribbling furiously to record the details of what I had begun to think of as my serial wet dream. My fingers trembled so violently, I dropped the pen. I clasped my hands tightly together and hunched my shoulders, weighed down by a sense of foreboding.

Once again I tried to recall the man's face.

Nothing. *Damn!* His face, the sensual line of his jaw, the lean, muscular chest—all of it was so clear in my dreams. Now, all I could see was that huge erection, his cock standing proud and dark amidst the thick mat of hair.

Had to be the hormones.

This time the dream had been different. We'd made contact, barely, but the shock of that brief touch still tingled through my fingertips, resided in my breasts, my aching cunt. It raced along my arm and settled deep in my gut.

I felt a vague heaviness, a deep sensual longing not usually associated with my nightmares—or my dreams—at least until this most recent series had begun.

I added a comment to that effect in my notes, not nearly as descriptive as it could have been, then placed the dog-eared tablet back on the table.

The digital clock blinked 5:28. There wasn't much point in trying to sleep for the half hour left to me.

The room seemed to sway, almost to pulsate in cadence with my thundering heart as I crawled from bed and toddled to the bathroom. I shouldn't have—I knew I must look like hell warmed over—but I stopped a minute to stare at my rumpled reflection in the mirror. My blond hair was matted and tangled, the shadows under my brown eyes looked like bruises.

My lips were swollen, as if from hours of kissing.

Yeah. Right. Dream on, sweetheart.

Hot flashes, serial nightmares-*slash*-wet dreams and a sexy guy I could never completely remember. *Double damn.* I turned around and started the shower, thankful for the extra settings on the shower massage.

This definitely had the makings of a really rotten day.

* * * * *

I adjusted my briefcase under my arm and bit my lips to keep from grinning. God, how I loved my work! No matter what my frame of mind, I couldn't help but pause every time I took that first of twenty-four marble steps up to the huge oak and brass front doors guarding the offices of San Francisco's premier newspaper, *The Bay Reporter.*

I was born to write news, the kind of news that exposes lies and uncovers secrets. I grew up in a tiny apartment off Nineteenth Avenue in what to me was heaven on earth—close enough to the Pacific to glimpse the sun setting over the ocean, only two blocks from Golden Gate Park.

I loved the city from the beginning, her cold, foggy summers and mild winters, the energy that's as much a part of her as the musical clang of cable car bells and her eclectic citizenry.

I felt a synchronicity with San Francisco's pulsing life from the very first, an inner sense of truth, a *knowing*, that never failed me. That sense led me to take that first marble step at *The Bay Reporter*, to take that step, and the next, and never look back.

I've covered the news beat for *The Bay Reporter* since my first break over twenty-five years ago, a riveting exposé on Elvis Presley's criminal ties. It was the story that got me out of the society pages and into hard news where I belong.

I love my work, the digging and interviewing, the bursts of intuition that often flower into facts, the hunches that pan out, even the rare ones that don't. The editor teases me about my *nose for news,* but I've sniffed my way into more stories than anyone else on staff.

It's that *knowing,* that sense that something is not quite as it should be—a feeling about people or situations that brings me up short, makes me stop and ponder and often leads me to information and conclusions without basis.

Then I'll dig deeper, follow leads that miraculously seem to come to me and eventually I find the proof that leads me right back to the conclusion I blithely *assumed* in the beginning. I don't understand it, but I'll take it.

After awhile, though, it's difficult to keep your perspective when your senses are constantly alive to every nuance, subtlety and trace of suspicion. Especially in a city where the rich and powerful exist in a rarefied atmosphere far above the law.

Which is why I didn't doubt my sources on my first big story one bit, or my instincts. There was something fishy about Elvis's death. It was too perfect, too *apropos*, almost as if it had been scripted for the six o'clock news.

I know I'm a cynic...an optimistic cynic, but still a cynic.

I was certain the King had faked his death, taken the money and run. It's just that I've never been able to prove it beyond a shadow of a doubt.

Still, it was one hell of a story. Most important, it got me to the news desk.

Elvis was still on my mind this particular day. It was either Elvis or obsessing over the erotic dream I'd had the night before. Elvis was a lot easier to deal with.

Unfortunately, the dream wouldn't go away. Today it appeared to have followed me, lying await for me in my subconscious.

It was late in the afternoon—I'd just plopped my butt down on the leather chair in front of my computer and was mulling over a feature story I'd been working on, my mind sort of wandering with ideas when the words on my computer screen suddenly appeared to sway and throb, almost as if the text within the monitor were alive.

I stared, hypnotized by the ebb and flow of text as it rushed and tumbled and finally found its cadence in perfect timing with my heartbeat. My heart. Beat. Beat. In, out, in-out...in...out...

Always in my dreams I've smelled the tang of saltwater, heard the rush of waves against the shore. Now there is silence, the deep, penetrating silence that comes with solid, sound-proofed walls and ceiling, silence further muted by heavy carpeting covering the floor.

My senses kick into high and I cast about, better to perceive my surroundings.

I must imagine the parameters of the room I am in. Darkness here is absolute. I see nothing. Hear nothing.

The air is motionless, no breeze or breath touches my skin.

My naked skin. I have come into this room as I entered the world, unadorned and naked. I touch my earlobe and realize the diamond stud is missing.

Kate Douglas

Suddenly I sense another presence, his *presence. I'm not surprised. Why else would I be here if not for him? I don't fear him, but there is a sense of fear entangled in his presence. I lower my hand, no longer concerned about the missing diamond.*

This time, there is no hesitation. Strong fingers grasp mine and the now-familiar shock of contact races up my arm as his hand pulls me closer. I cannot see him — the darkness is absolute.

I can smell his body, a warm, masculine combination of healthy sweat and aftershave. I lean against his chest and feel the crinkly mat of hair tickle my cheek. It's real — no fanciful illusion of my dreams. Almost whimpering with pleasure, I inhale, a deep, drugging breath filled with his scent.

I can taste him. I run my tongue over his nipple and the lean muscles of his chest quiver beneath my hands. His soft groan invites me to taste more.

The sound of his need banishes the sense of dread, of foreboding that has lingered abut us.

I use my tongue to blaze a trail from his left nipple to his groin. I start with his heartbeat, licking, laving the flat nipple, the ridge of pectoral muscle. By the time I am on my knees, his hands are fisted in my hair, his taut thighs rigid beneath my stroking fingers.

I caress his buttocks, pulling him close to my mouth. I don't need to see his rampant erection to recognize his cock. Big, thick, the head rounded like a succulent fruit ripe for the plucking.

I wrap my lips around the end and use my tongue to find the sensitive ridges and contours. His hips jerk at my touch and I comply, opening my mouth as wide as I can, taking him as deep as possible.

He slides easily into my mouth, filling but not gagging me as I'd expected. Instead, his lovely cock slips in and out, deeper with each thrust until I swallow him completely, without effort.

My lips clamp tightly around the base of his penis. Impossibly, I have taken all of him. I continue to caress his buttocks, my fingers tightening around his muscular ass to hold him captive. His fingers clench my hair, practically ripping it from my scalp and he groans aloud. I answer him with my own moan. The sound vibrates through my mouth, against the length of him.

There is power in me, the power of seductress, of wanton. I am an enchantress, a seeker of pleasure. This knowledge frees me, emboldens me. Slowly I withdraw my lips from his cock, licking and tasting his entire length.

My fingers slide around his tense thighs and I cup his testicles in my hands. Nestled in a thick tangle of hair, they fill my palms, heavy, hot. Gently I caress them with my fingertips.

I hear his breath catch in his throat.

I am wet and pulsing. Needy. As my tongue lifts a tiny drop of fluid from the end of his penis, I feel its answering droplets flowing down my leg, preparing the way for him. I blow a draft of cool air against the silken head of his cock, then reach down and run a finger between my own legs. He grabs my hand. Pulling me to my feet, he wraps his lips around my fingers and suckles them.

His tongue sweeps against my palm and my knees buckle.

Suddenly, sound disturbs me, shatters the darkness lush with passion, shatters the dream.

The phone rang again.

I stared at it for a moment, trying to remember exactly what one does with a ringing phone.

"Nita Franklin, news," I said. My voice was breathless, as if I'd just run up three flights of stairs. My brain felt divided. Half of it functioning as only half a brain would, the other half pleading to go back to the dream.

The voice on the other end banished my strangely erotic fantasy. Smooth and fine, the cultured baritone sent chills up my arms and conjured sensual images of tuxedoes, bittersweet chocolate and fine brandy.

My dream lover had never spoken. Not once. He would sound exactly like this man.

A shiver raced along my arms.

My well-clothed arms. I shook the remnants of the dream out of my mind. The sensual images scattered like so much chaff in the wind.

"Ms. Franklin?"

Just that, my last name. I caught myself licking my lips in anticipation. I could still taste the sweetly salty drop I'd licked from the end of that pulsing cock in my fantasy.

Suddenly, my senses kicked into overdrive. They'd screamed at me this morning when I was caught in the stranglehold of my dreams, again, just moments before when I'd taken that throbbing, rock-solid piece of...

Who *was* this man?

"Yes?" I sat up straight. *Get a grip, girl!*

"Martin Hawley, Hawley Enterprises." A pause, giving me time to be impressed. I was, but I wasn't about to let him know.

"What can I do for you?" Sweet and to the point. He'd never know my nerves had flown into overdrive, not suspect I was already thinking of plenty of things *he* could do for *me.* Things he might have done if the damned phone hadn't interrupted my...no. I wasn't ready to go there. Not yet.

My dreams were dreams. No more, no less than the frustrated fantasies of a sexually deprived, menopausal broad.

"That series you wrote, the one on the import/export trade? I'm interested in one of the businessmen you interviewed."

His subject matter banished the fantasy entirely. Businessmen, ha! Thugs, maybe. The hairs on the back of my neck prickled. *Why?* Hawley Enterprises was big, but local. They handled accounts and investments for firms around the Bay, as well as fundraising for the Metro Museum. I'd seen Hawley in public service commercials with his daughter.

His tall, slim, outrageously gorgeous daughter.

"What exactly do you want?" I asked "The articles are fairly self-explanatory, but..."

"I need to reach Mr. Delgado, one of the gentlemen you interviewed."

Gentleman? Who the hell did he think he was kidding? Delgado was a Grade A rat. Why would Hawley want to contact a crook like Delgado and why didn't he just call the man's office, the way I had?

Which is exactly what I told Hawley. Along with the fact I never divulge source information, even if it's just a number out of the phone book. That's not my style.

"Ms. Franklin, we need to talk." I sensed desperation in his voice, something I hadn't noticed before. My curiosity, along with that damned sixth sense, was screaming out loud, so I named a coffee shop across the street and down the block from my office. I told him I'd be there in fifteen minutes.

I saved the story I was working on, a fluff piece on near death experiences. Before the screen went blank, I stared at the text a moment, daring it to go into its little ebb and flow routine. The words stayed put. The screen went dark. I headed to the restroom to wash the grime off my hands.

It never ceases to amaze me how dirty I manage to get, working in a perfectly clean office behind a sterile looking computer. I guess I'm just rumpled by nature.

I scrubbed my hands and suddenly realized I was combing my hair and putting on fresh lipstick. Definitely not my style.

I've never been one of those women who wear make-up like armor, hiding behind the artifice for an extra burst of confidence. Of course, my mother is constantly reminding me that's probably why I'm still single at forty-eight—one more good reason not to visit dear old Mom all that often.

I glanced over my shoulder before I shoved the lipstick back into my purse. I'd never hear the end of it if anyone on the staff saw me primping for a meeting with a guy like Hawley.

Thank whatever gods protected me, no one had entered my office while I'd been in the throes of my serial wet dream. Shaking my head, I marveled at my own lack of control.

Already I was breaking my rules about powerful, good-looking men, but that voice had gotten my attention. That, and the knowledge he was very much a part of the damned nightmares I'd been having.

Of course, last night's hadn't exactly been a nightmare, at least not until my dream-self took a tumble off the cliff. No, just dredging up the image of that gorgeous body, those long, lean legs and the improbably long, thick cock between them, made me hot.

I licked my lips, then realized that was exactly what I'd done in the dream last night. Licked my lips and wished I'd been licking him. Today, only minutes before, I'd gotten my wish.

I opened my mouth wide and ran my finger along my lips, smearing my fresh lipstick. My jaws ached. My mouth felt as if it had been stretched just a bit too far.

I thought of that improbably large cock, recalled how easily I had taken it down my throat.

Desire flooded me with an almost painful intensity. I grabbed the porcelain sink for balance, suddenly caught up in the vivid images that seemed to have suddenly taken over both my sleeping and waking moments.

Last night I'd only been able to focus on his face, on the mysterious, mesmerizing eyes hidden beneath black brows. Why, now, was I almost preternaturally aware of the more earthy aspects of the mystery man, of his scent, his taste, his muscular legs and buttocks, his long, thick cock—the heavy testicles surrounded by a dense forest of rough hair?

Aware of him as if I truly *had* experienced him?

I trembled, an involuntary shudder that was purely sexual in nature.

Had to be hormones.

The dreams had begun almost a month ago, about the time I'd finished up the Delgado story. At first they'd been vague images, a bit sensual, frightening at times, but nothing definite. Only in the past few days had they grown so distinct, the sensuality more compelling, more erotic.

More demanding.

The eroticism, though, had been garbed in dread and dismay. Passion alone, at least until today, couldn't overshadow the sense of foreboding, the feeling I must pay heed to some undefined warning.

Today's experience had been the unique among the unusual. If the phone hadn't interrupted, I fully believed we might actually have had real, honest-to-god-down-and-dirty sex.

That kind of dream, I figured I could live with.

Of course, since the dreams were usually accompanied by a hot flash, I should have blamed them on too few hormones, too much caffeine and a non-existent sex life.

Then again, if the dreams continued, my sex life wouldn't be so bad. The fantasy, so far, certainly outstripped reality.

Reality often sucks the big one. I have a hard time believing I'm as old as I am. I feel like a twenty-year-old most of the time, not forty-eight and starting *the change*.

All in all, though, life is not bad for this old broad. I'd not only written a potential Pulitzer with my exposé on Delgado, I still looked damned good.

For an old broad.

Putting the dreams aside, I blew myself a reflected kiss in the mirror and pushed the hair back from my face, over my left ear. My earring sparkled beneath the garish fluorescent light. Suddenly recalling an incident in my daydream, I brushed back the hair on my right, exposing my other ear.

My favorite diamond stud was missing.

A foreboding shiver raced along my spine. I pulled my hair back on both sides of my face and stared at my reflection.

Left ear, properly adorned with a diamond.

Right ear naked.

There was a logical reason for the missing stud. A perfectly logical reason.

I just didn't know it yet.

I checked my watch, noted I would barely make it on time and headed out for my meeting with Hawley. I convinced myself I'd probably find the earring on my pillow at home. By the time I sauntered across the street and headed down the block I was feeling kind of cocky.

I shoulda known better. The minute I get cocky, well, that's when it hits the fan.

I walked into Sallie's right on time and spotted Martin Hawley already sitting in one of the booths. My breath caught on a sigh and I stared.

The TV spots didn't do him justice. Neither had my dreams—there was no doubt in my mind this was *the man*. I might not have been able to recall the distinctive features of his face when I first awoke that morning and I hadn't seen his face at all this afternoon, but here—*now*—in person, I knew.

The same man invading my thoughts night after fearful night, the same man who'd clenched his fingers in my hair barely half an hour ago and groaned with unspent passion while I sucked on his cock…

That same man was sitting at a booth in Sallie's, staring out the window.

I wondered what he'd been doing—I glanced down at my watch—nineteen minutes ago?

He was something else in person, long narrow face, thick gray eyebrows over dark blue, deep-set eyes, a strong nose with an eagle's hook.

The face of a predator.

I took a quick look along the length of him, disappointed the table hid the best part, though his legs stretched out, long and lean, into the aisle.

I consoled myself with the fact I'd seen him naked.

Standing there, I imagined those long legs tangled with mine. Suddenly I realized he'd glanced away from the window to study me. There was a brief flash of recognition, a narrowing of the eyes, tightening of the lips. Then it was my turn for the once-over.

I wasn't certain I liked it.

Not that he visually undressed me—nothing that crude. He didn't have to. My heart practically stopped in my chest and I struggled to swallow past the lump in my throat.

The knowing look in his eye gave him away—he'd shared the same dreams I had, experienced the same erotic need that had awakened me on so many mornings.

Where had he been twenty minutes ago? Where had Martin Hawley *really* been when I'd knelt between his legs and taken him in my mouth?

I shivered with the physical memory of the unfulfilled passion coursing through my body.

No, there was no need for Martin Hawley to demean either of us by something as crude as visually undressing me. I didn't even need one of my infamous hunches to know he'd already seen me naked as a jaybird.

I held my chin high and looked right into those haunting blue eyes. He read me like an open book. When he finished, he knew too damned much.

More of my attitude slipped, along with my confidence. What in the hell was going on here? I walked up to him, surreptitiously checking to make sure I was actually still clothed, introduced myself and scooted across the cracked vinyl seat into the booth.

At least I managed that maneuver without tripping over my own feet. Something about this man made me feel like a gawky teenager and it wasn't just the residual power of the dreams.

"Okay, Hawley," I said, my tone confrontational. "You somehow manage to get through six blocks of San Francisco rush hour traffic in under fifteen minutes, all for a phone number you can get out of the book? What gives?"

He glanced away, then tilted his head and looked me directly in the eye. That bird of prey image hovered between us. He was taking my measure and it was all I could do not to squirm in my seat.

So much for the hard-boiled news reporter.

"I had you investigated," he said. "Nothing personal, you understand, but I had to know if I can trust you."

There really is no answer to an opening like that. I returned his pragmatic stare with one of my own.

Silence stretched between us, taut, filled with the familiar tension of my dreams. He blinked, took a deep breath, obviously reached a conclusion. "I have to trust you." He sounded regretful. He paused, then nailed me with that predator's stare. "Do you dream, Ms Franklin?"

What the hell? Talk about catching a woman off balance! I knew he didn't expect an answer. My deep blush must have told him all he wanted to know.

He was obviously satisfied with my silence.

He nodded once, a tacit acknowledgment of something shared. Something neither of us appeared willing, or able, to voice. His eyes closed and he bowed his head. For a moment he reminded me of a man in prayer. When he raised his head, his composure had shattered.

"My daughter..." His voice broke; he coughed, cleared his throat. When he spoke again it was a mere whisper of sound. "Melinda...my daughter's life...help me."

I stared at him, speechless. What could I say? Melinda Hawley, his gorgeous, raven-haired daughter, reportedly as sweet and kind as she was beautiful. In danger?

I put my notebook away. Obviously it was making the man nervous.

"I'm listening." I spread my hands out on the table. For one brief moment I felt as if I were surrendering.

He took a sip of coffee, then carefully set the mug back on the table. His fingers cradled the heavy restaurant pottery as if it were a religious icon. I caught myself staring at those exquisitely long fingers, the neatly trimmed nails...staring and imagining them touching me, slipping in and out of...

"You started this," he said, accusing me. I snapped to attention, his fingers relegated to the back burners of my mind. "My company was hired to audit Delgado's books after *The Bay Reporter* ran your exposé. We found discrepancies right away, nothing major, but enough to send up a red flag. About a week into the audit, I got a call. Typical heavy breather, no ID. Before I could hang up, the caller warned me to back off the audit. His voice was disguised. The threat wasn't. It was really quite explicit."

He glanced out the window. A chill raced along my spine and I thought of the call I'd gotten a few nights ago. Heavy breathing, no voice. At the time, I figured it was some guy jacking off on the other end. I'd hung up and forgotten about it. Until now.

"I reported the threat to the DA," Hawley said, his gorgeous hands still wrapped tightly around the mug. "He'd gotten the same call. So had every other member of the auditing team. Every last one of them. We've all got unlisted numbers, Ms. Franklin."

He raised his cup to take a sip. A little of his coffee sloshed out of the half-empty cup and he carefully placed the mug back on the table, methodically wiping at the small puddle with a paper napkin. "I should have listened," he muttered, as much to himself as to me. "We went on with the audit, no more threats, business as usual. Until last night."

Even choked with emotion, Martin Hawley remained the predator. Frustrated, momentarily impotent, his taut frame still radiated power. Energy danced in the air between us.

"They've got Melinda." His shoulders tensed, straining at the expensive suit. "Either I convince the DA to call off the investigation or they're going to let her die. She's buried somewhere—somewhere they said I'll never find her. The bastards are pumping in barely enough oxygen to keep her alive. I either," he paused, closed his eyes to whatever demons haunted him, then took a deep breath. "I either *adjust* the audit or they cut off her air. It's as simple as that."

Suddenly his broad shoulders slumped and his hands trembled. He was losing the iron control that'd been holding him together, exhausting the rage giving him strength. Without thinking I reached across the chipped Formica table and covered his hand with my own.

It happened again. The same burst of energy, the elemental shock of contact I'd experienced in my dreams. The reaction was instantaneous—suddenly my nipples were tight and hard, my breasts sensitive to every seam and stitch in my bra, my utilitarian nylon panties wet.

I blinked, refocused, found my bearings once more. But I left my hand there, covering his, and wondered if he noticed anything at all.

"Mr. Hawley, I have no idea what I can offer that will help save your daughter, but whatever you need from me..."

He shuddered. For a brief moment my heart soared. *He's feeling the same thing I am!*

Then I felt like a total jerk. Worry was making him shiver, not any overwhelming lust for an old broad with hormone problems.

My opinion of the man underwent a rapid change. I'd never had a kid but he obviously loved his and I could tell his daughter's abduction tore him apart. All his money and power couldn't save him from this terrible pain.

He rolled his hand under mine, grasped my fingers firmly in his. "You know more about Delgado than anyone." He squeezed my hand for emphasis. "You've been inside his operation. Whitaker was afraid you'd end up on Delgado's hit list because of your story, but he was glad you were working on it. He said his hands were tied because of regulations. Yours aren't."

Hawley released my hand, making his point. I'd known the pudgy little DA for years and was actually pretty fond of the guy. He could be a real jerk, but he took his job seriously. Sometimes Billy Whitaker got frustrated enough to break rules. I've always admired a person who'll put his job on the line for the sake of justice.

"I think Delgado's got Melinda down by the docks." Hawley linked his fingers. The joints cracked. He looked down at his hands as if surprised by the sound, then sighed loudly, a great whoosh of breath encompassing the emotions I knew he struggled to control.

"I heard a tape of her voice, crying, begging me for help. She called me *Daddy*. She hasn't called me *Daddy* since she was a little girl, back when her mother was still alive. God, don't let those be the last words I hear from her!"

Rubbing his hand roughly across his face, Hawley ruthlessly continued. "I may have heard a foghorn in the background. I'm not sure..." He tightened his right hand into a fist. "I'm just not sure!" He pounded the table in frustration. "I've got to find her. She's all I have left..."

I thought of his money, his beautiful offices, that gorgeous home in Tiburon overlooking the city, the bay and the Golden Gate Bridge...

"You've been there, Ms. Franklin. You're going to help me search Delgado's warehouses."

Right. At your command.

I had no choice, really. I hadn't had a choice from the beginning. A beginning that had started with those odd, unnerving, erotic dreams.

We went back to my office and I shoved the research notes on near death experiences out of the way. Lately it seemed everything I wrote was about death, even when the people lived to tell about it.

I closed the door, thankful once again I rated more than a cube after all my years on staff, and pulled a thick stack of folders and a half-empty bottle of good Irish whiskey out of the filing cabinet. Without a word, Martin handed me a couple of paper cups from the water dispenser near the window. I splashed a healthy shot of booze into each one.

I divided the folders into two piles and put one of the stacks in front of him. By now we were on a first name basis and when he thanked me I liked the way my name rolled off his tongue.

He didn't mention the dreams again. He didn't have to. They hovered between us, silent specters hanging motionless in the shadows, their presence a clear reminder of passion, of life, of what we shared. Somehow, we had prepared for this moment. Knowing that gave me a burst of confidence, renewed my sense of self.

Martin grabbed a chair and sorted through the papers, sipping slowly at his whiskey. I did the same. Somewhere, buried in six months of research, was a clue that might lead us to Melinda.

Chapter Two

ॐ

We'd been at it a couple of hours and the half bottle of whiskey was long gone when my sixth sense kicked in. I held up a page of notes about an old granary belonging, in a roundabout manner, to Delgado. I'd actually been inside, at least until one of Delgado's henchmen realized I was a reporter and *escorted* me out the door.

"I've got a feeling about this one," I said, unwilling to explain how my hunches so often pan out. Martin looked over my notes and shrugged his shoulders. It was already dark outside, and sitting here wasn't helping us find Melinda.

"Okay," he said. He reached for the phone and called Whitaker. The DA wasn't in, but Martin left a message on the machine telling him where we were headed and why. I slipped into the restroom and changed into an old pair of running shoes and pulled a dark sweatshirt over my blouse. I held up the sweatpants, then tossed them aside.

My slacks were raw silk and linen, expensive as hell, but so dark a gray they'd look almost black. Besides, they did a lot more for my figure than the sweats. So did the cute little bikini panties I switched into.

I tossed the plain white nylon underpants into my briefcase, snapped the clasp shut and brushed my hands along my hips, unable to suppress a grin. Perfect attire for the well-dressed cat burglar, especially one accompanied by someone as sexy and sensual as Martin Hawley.

Then I thought of Melinda, buried God knows where, and my grin faded. I skipped fresh lipstick as penance. I did run a brush through my hair, though I felt guilty as hell primping even that much.

It took us about twenty minutes to reach the docks. I parked my faded Toyota in deep shadows near an overpass. We were less than a block from our destination, an old concrete and brick warehouse built back in the twenties. I'd heard stories about this place, how it had been used to hide smuggled booze during prohibition.

It stood like a towering monolith here at the edge of the city, marking that no-man's land between the buildings and the bay. We had no proof Melinda was anywhere near but my senses were buzzing and Martin followed me without question.

Fog shrouded the warehouse with a blanket thick enough to trap the glow of the single streetlight at the corner. The structure itself was completely dark, its windows boarded over. The stench of diesel fuel and rotting fish warred with the tang of salt. Here in the shadows, silence folded in upon itself. Our footsteps sounded strangely out of place as I led Martin across the cracked, rubbish-strewn parking lot.

He followed me without question until I stopped, turned and shrugged my shoulders. My senses were still alive and buzzing, but the solid wall of brick and concrete in front of us offered little hope of entrance. I wasn't about to announce our presence by heading around to the dock side, where the clang of metal and occasional shout announced others were awake this night.

The only entrance visible from this side, a rusting staircase that wound up and around the building before disappearing into the fog, was obviously too far corroded to bear our weight.

Martin glanced up at the rusted metal then suddenly leaned over and kissed me. Shock brought my heart to a standstill, stopped my breath and coiled like a deep, smoldering fire in my womb. I wrapped my arms around his neck and stood up on my toes.

My mouth opened for his. His tongue stroked my lips and my teeth, finally found its way inside to tease and tickle my mouth and tongue. I pressed my hips forward until I found him, his erection long and hard against his belly. I forgot fear, forgot every reason we were here in the warehouse district, not home in my bed exploring this strange connection.

He scattered warm little kisses along my chin, down my throat. I arched my back, bared my throat to give him access. Finally, with a soft little sigh I hoped was regret, he stopped. Holding my jaw in both hands, he stared deep into my eyes.

I saw promise in his. "For luck," he whispered. Suddenly he stepped around me and ducked beneath the stairs. He disappeared entirely into the shadows. Seconds later he whistled, a sharp hiss meant for my ears alone.

Still trembling from his sensual assault, I scooted nervously into the darkness, close beside him, inhaling the scent of his aftershave along with the more pungent odor of nervous sweat and healthy male.

The sweat could have been mine...I was terrified, hunched there in the dark beneath the rusted stairs, frightened as much by my *sense* of danger as the actual circumstances.

Martin tapped my shoulder and pointed to a small door tucked up against the building. I'm convinced the Fates smile on fools...by all rights the door should have been locked, but when Martin tugged at the handle a ragged whisper of metal on concrete echoed eerily in the still evening. We both froze.

When nothing jumped out of the dark and attacked, I pulled my little penlight out of my pocket. Martin looked at it and frowned.

"Is that all the light you have?"

Granted, it wasn't much, but it was better than what he'd brought.

Nothing.

I said as much.

Suddenly, he looked bereft, as if his inattention to that one detail might cost Melinda her life.

Wordlessly, I handed the flashlight over to him.

He clicked it on. The pale glow barely reached the ground.

We inched along the wall, running our fingertips across the damp concrete surface to keep our bearings.

My hunch that Melinda was nearby grew stronger, but so did another feeling, a disturbing sense we weren't alone. I dared not make a sound to warn Martin, unwilling to announce our presence any further. Martin moved soundlessly about five paces ahead of me, a dark silhouette of leashed power barely visible in the feeble glow from the penlight.

Suddenly a huge shadow blocked even that pale glimmer.

Martin grunted and disappeared in darkness. I dropped to the floor and rolled in the opposite direction, banging my head on something hard and metallic before coming to rest in what felt like a jumble of wires and baled paper.

The overhead lights flashed on, momentarily blinding me, but I was partially concealed by the untidy stacks of bales and boxes. I took advantage of the sudden noise and confusion to inch my way deeper into the pile. An excited mixture of English and Spanish echoed off the walls, but none of the voices belonged to Martin.

Then I heard Delgado. No mistaking that voice, the one that reminded me of Peter Lorre with a head cold. "Hawley, you fool," he sneered. I heard a thump and a groan. "You just signed two death warrants...yours and your daughter's."

Another dull thud, a cry of pain. "Eddie, turn off the bitch's air and throw this jerk into the storeroom. We'll do him later. I want him alive at least ten more minutes, long enough to know his kid's dead."

Melinda! She *was* here. But where? I heard a door slam at the far end of the building, then silence. I had no idea where they'd taken Martin *or* hidden his daughter.

I had to believe Martin would be okay. Right now, I was Melinda's only chance.

Working my way around the bales as quickly and silently as possible, I reached a row of doors evenly spaced along one wall. I tried the handle on the first one. Locked! I tried the second, my hands slipping on the cold steel handle. Two more to go and Melinda was running out of time!

I reached for the third, felt the handle give just as blunt fingers grabbed me by the throat. Grabbed me and tightened with almost inhuman strength.

I've tried to be logical about what happened next—my journalistic mind works best with logic—but it's not easy to explain in a logical manner.

I remember trying to scream, but I made no sound. I scratched and clawed at my attacker's hands with all my strength. I can still feel the pain of my fingernails tearing, the growing pressure on my throat. The room dimming, then utter darkness.

Suddenly I was floating outside my body. There was no pain, no sense of fear as I watched myself hanging limply in the strangling grasp of a muscular, dark-haired man.

Then I was racing through a dark tunnel while some odd little part of my mind recalled the article I'd been writing, the research I'd done. I remember mentally patting myself on the back, knowing I'd been right on target in my descriptions of near death experiences.

But was this *near* death or that final journey? I felt no fear, only regret and curiosity—regret I'd not have the chance to know Martin better, not ever experience those long legs tangled in mine, those beautiful hands touching, exploring...as for the questions? They faded in a heartbeat.

Heartbeat. Heart beat. Heart. Beat.

Pounding rhythm of my heart.

Beat of my heart, beat of my heart, rush of my blood, beating, beating with the speed of the wind, the sound of the rushing wind and rushing blood until I was speed and wind, accelerating faster, ever faster, rushing headlong toward a brilliant shimmer of light. The velocity – exhilarating, the goal – seductive.

I could not deny the call of the light.

Figures appeared, familiar faces out of my past.

Family, friends long gone...there was the Grateful Dead's Jerry Garcia, guitar in hand, and I swear the guy he was talking to looked just like Elvis.

I'd been wrong about the King. He hadn't faked his death after all.

I wanted to stop, say hello, apologize to Elvis for my woefully inaccurate story. But the seductive lure of the light increased, coupled with a sense of undefined urgency. Undefined until a slender figure stepped into my path and halted my headlong rush.

Melinda Hawley grabbed my arm. I felt her life force, strong and pulsing in her grasp. Her dark eyes pleaded with me. "Go back," she said. "Please. For me. For my father. For yourself. It's not our time. You're the only one who can save us. Open the fourth door. There's a panel hidden behind the filing cabinet. Move the cabinet and press the upper right corner of the panel. Hurry, please!"

I looked into her eyes—looked into them and saw her soul and the soul of her father. Saw my own reflection staring back at me, saw the loneliness that was my life.

Saw my future in the choices before me. Follow the light, give way to the beguiling lure of oblivion, or return to the torment of Delgado's henchman, to pain, to destiny unknown.

Return to a chance with Martin Hawley.

Hell, what kind of a choice was that?

Suddenly I was back in my body, my throat hurt like hell and little Billy Whitaker, the pudgy DA, was leaning over me, blowing air into my lungs. He certainly wasn't the prince I'd choose to kiss me back to life, but at least he got the job done.

Gasping, wrenching my face away from his, I grabbed his arm, ordered him to help me up. Damn, it hurt to talk! "Quick, the fourth door. Melinda's behind the fourth door!" The harsh whisper I managed to croak out must have made some kind of sense. He didn't hesitate even though I doubt he understood a word I said.

Whitaker didn't waste time on the locked handle. He slammed against the door, splintering the frame and exposing a beautiful, expensively furnished office, completely out of place within the boundaries of the dingy warehouse.

Still reeling from lack of oxygen, I stumbled through the door after him. Together we shoved the cabinet aside. The panel was right where it should be. When I pressed the upper right corner, a seam opened in the perfect hardwood floor, exposing a doorway into a hidden, coffin-like room.

Melinda was there, curled up in the fetal position. Bill jumped down into the box and shook her. She didn't respond. He leaned over and, just as he had done for me, blew into her mouth, filling her lungs with life-giving air. Thank God the little guy knew his first aid. I held my breath, knowing she had to live, knowing it wasn't her time to die.

Her slender body shuddered and her dark eyes opened. "Nita, you made it," was all she said before her eyes closed again. But she was breathing on her own and I gave myself permission to crumple in a heap on the floor.

Martin caught me before my head hit the hardwood, then spotted Melinda and dropped to his knees, still holding me tightly against his chest. "We're too late," he whispered. His voice cracked as he rocked me. I wrapped my arms around him and told him everything was gonna be fine.

About then Bill looked up at me, his face a mask of curiosity, and said, "Nita, I didn't know you and Melinda knew each other."

* * * * *

Somehow, once the emergency technicians decided Melinda belonged in the hospital for observation but I didn't, Martin and I ended up at his ritzy little bachelor pad in the Marina District. He kept the place for those nights when he didn't want to cross the bridge to his palatial home on the far side of the bay.

I stood in the darkness before a huge double-paned window and watched the lights from the cars streaming across the Golden Gate. I wondered if Martin kept this elegant row house for the nights he wanted to be alone with a woman, since Melinda still lived at home.

"No," he said.

I turned and took the glass of brandy he handed to me. "I didn't say anything." I frowned, too tired to argue. Light from the street lamp below glinted off his high cheekbones, outlined the sensual curve of his lips "No, what?"

"No. There's no other woman."

"How did you even know I wondered?" I sipped the brandy, remembered my first impression of Martin's voice. *Bittersweet chocolate and fine brandy.* Was it only this afternoon?

"I know much about you, Nita Franklin." He cupped my face in those long fingers. His palms were firm and warm. His fingertips lightly massaged my temples. "I know you've come to me in my dreams, a succubus there to steal my soul. But you didn't steal it, did you? No. You've saved it."

He leaned forward and kissed me. The kiss he'd begun earlier at the warehouse. The kiss he'd almost taken in my dreams.

Imposing even in passion, he drew the air from my lungs and all conscious thought from my mind. The glass of brandy tipped from my lifeless fingers and shattered on the elegant Italian marble floor.

I heard the sound as if from a great distance, muffled beneath the pounding of my heart, the steady beat of his.

He lifted me, his strong arms beneath my back and knees, our lips still connected in a sensual exploration that sent my senses flying. He carried me to the white leather couch and sat with me across his lap.

His hand traced the curve of my calf and I was inordinately thankful I'd worn the silk and linen slacks instead of sweatpants. The fabric slipped beneath his fingers, the slick rustling shimmer a counterpoint to the soft, breathy moans escaping my lips.

He reached the zipper at the side of my slacks, lowered it and slipped his hand inside. His fingers deftly traced my belly, found my navel then trailed lower, slipping beneath the elastic of my bikini cut briefs until they tangled in the soft brush of hair at my mound.

His arm supported my back as I arched my hips, inviting him closer. One finger trailed sweetly over my greedy clitoris, circled it a couple of times then slipped deeper, into the moisture gathering there at his command. He moved much too slowly, mere fractions of a millimeter, until I groaned in frustration.

He swallowed the sound and appeased me with the slightest advance, dipping another finger between my labia. I felt the tissues swelling, softening for him.

He found a rhythm then, a sweet tempo that had me bucking my hips in counterpoint as he played me.

It was one damned, short song. My climax slammed into me before I even had a chance to wallow in the foreplay. I cried out and buried my head against his shoulder. He thrust his fingers deep inside, my muscles clenched around his hand as if trying their damnedest to hold on to him.

He chuckled, nudged my head back with his forehead and kissed my chin. His fingers were still deep inside, my vagina still clenching, releasing, clenching. My mouth was wide open, sucking in as much air as I could get. I should have felt like a beached salmon, but the look in his eyes made me beautiful.

He held me a moment longer, then slipped his fingers from me, sliding over my clit on the way out. I jumped at the contact and he had the nerve to tickle that blasted pack of nerve endings one more time.

"For good measure," he whispered. Then he took his fingers, the ones he'd just fucked me with, still glistening with my juices, and slipped them between his lips.

I almost came again, watching him lick my essence off those long, slim fingers. He'd done the same in my dream this afternoon, suckling my fingers after I'd touched myself.

I'd never known a man who found my taste desirable, never appreciated the complete eroticism of the act.

He lifted me as if I weighed nothing, helped me turn so that I straddled his waist. Then he undressed me. I tried to help him with his shirt, but my hands trembled with unspent passion. I wanted him.

He unbuttoned my blouse and slipped it over my shoulders, carefully undid my bra. The clasp in the front parted easily and the soft cups fell away, but he caught both breasts in his hands and supported them, staring.

The power of his eyes pulled my darkened nipples into tight, aching kernels of pure desire. He rubbed his thumbs lightly across the tips and I felt a spiral of heat course from breasts to groin.

His hands slipped over my ribcage, leaving my breasts alone and bereft until he hooked his fingers in the loosened waistband of my slacks. I stretched up on my knees as Martin shoved the slacks over my hips.

With a quick twist and a squirm, I raised up enough that he managed to get the slacks and my briefs off my legs with a minimum of fuss. The minute the fabric shimmered to the ground, he took the advantage, grasping my rear in both his hands and lifting me closer to his mouth.

I wanted to watch, wanted to study the intense gleam in his eyes, the slight fluttering at the side of his nostrils, the clenched jaw as he fought his own need.

I was doing this to him. Me, forty-eight-year-old Nita Franklin, the menopausal broad who hadn't been laid in over a year. Merely by being here, being female, being the woman Martin Hawley had chosen, I was the one responsible for the catch in his breath, the obvious tenting at the front of his loose slacks.

I closed my eyes. Closed them against the need I saw on his face, the desire so intense it was too personal to observe. Closed them just as his lips found my breast, as his tongue encircled my engorged nipple and drew it into his mouth.

I moaned. It had to be me. Martin had too much class to moan with need and demand. Then my eyes fluttered open and I saw the stark desire on his face, his high cheekbones and sharp jaw line all shadows and angles in the darkened room.

He lifted me off his lap and slowly stretched me out along the couch. The muscles in his arms trembled as if he fought himself for control.

He brushed the hair back from my forehead and I saw my own naked hunger in his eyes. I grabbed his hand and kissed the palm, running my tongue along the thick pad at the base of his thumb then drawing his middle finger between my lips, suckling it.

Martin grasped my chin with his fingers and moaned. There was no doubt in my mind this time. The sound was his. I slipped his finger from my mouth and licked his palm once more, turning him free.

He slipped lower, kissing his way down my belly, across my naked thighs, his tongue leaving a damp trail leading to the crease where groin met thigh.

He kneaded my buttocks with his strong hands, lifting me ever closer to his mouth. There was no subtlety in his approach. He lightly kissed my mons, then wrapped his lips around my clitoris as if it were a nipple made for suckling.

Gently, so gently I wanted to cry, he suckled that tiny nubbin, soothing it with his tongue, his warm lips an exquisite caress more intimate than anything I'd ever experienced. My entire being centered in that one spot so that I was only peripherally aware of his fingers.

Kneading, massaging, rubbing, his fingers growing ever closer to that other nerve center, his touch so stealthy I was barely aware when he dipped into my vagina, covering his fingers with moisture, using that slick lubricant I knew he favored to rub silky rings around my anus.

He suckled my clit, once more finding a rhythm between lips and fingers. My legs, drawn up, knees bent to allow him full access, fell open even further. My fingers somehow found themselves entangled in the thick hair tumbling over his forehead.

Once more I felt myself peaking, the coil of need tightening my muscles, pulling a low wail from somewhere deep in my chest. Suddenly, his tongue speared me, as did one of his slim fingers, the duel penetration rocketing me over the edge.

Gasping, muscles front and rear caught in the spasm of climax, I still thought of the cliff, thought of the lonely tumble I'd taken in my dreams.

Twice more I'd taken the fall alone.

Next time, Martin was going with me.

He grinned at me, the powerful, lazy, sexy grin of a man in absolute control.

For now.

I didn't give him a chance to protest. Even though my arms and legs felt like lead, I managed to sit up and tug his shirt off his shoulders. My next move was to slip his pants down his slim hips.

He was older than me by two years. I'd read the bio, knew all the stats, but they didn't do justice to the lean, muscular body I found buried beneath that fine fabric. The mat of hair covering his chest was iron gray but the happy trail running from his navel to his groin was still black as night.

Even in the semi-darkness of the room, I recognized his impossibly long cock. I'd seen Martin's face in photos before, had admired his well-dressed body on the evening news and at the occasional event where I'd attended as a reporter, but I'd never seen his cock, other than in my dreams.

Just as he'd never seen me naked...other than his dreams. My hunch, earlier today in the restaurant, had been right on the mark.

Was it only today?

I knew this man, more intimately than I should.

Knew him with a sense of the inevitable.

How? I'll never understand, but it was truly Martin who had visited me all those nights, Martin who had mesmerized me then as he did now.

I leaned over and drew the soft tip of his penis between my lips. I recalled doing this earlier today, when I'd been more concerned with fit than flavor. He tasted...wonderful. How do you describe the flavors of passion? Of desire? Of dreams fulfilled? I wrapped my fingers around the base of his cock, steadying this elegant beast, and took him into my mouth.

My tongue read the tastes and textures of velvet and steel, silk and bone. Soft and so sweet, powerful, potent. His testicles were drawn up tight between his legs, but I lapped my way down his cock and drew each one into my mouth, tongued the solid mass within, suckled each ball and learned its shape and texture.

Martin lay back, one knee bent and resting against the soft cushions on the couch, the other leg over the edge, foot firmly planted on the floor. His hands lightly massaged my scalp. He was obviously still in complete control, even as he gave me free access to do with him as I wished.

I wished to do a lot.

Even after two sensational climaxes, passion still simmered, hot and untamped, in my soul. I wanted more of him, more of the tastes and textures of his body.

I took Martin's straining cock back into my mouth and kneaded his hard buttocks much as he'd massaged mine. I lifted his hips and built a rhythm, my tongue, teeth and lips adding texture and the occasional nip for emphasis.

My fingers found the crease of his butt, the tight, puckered muscle filled with nerve endings. I massaged that as I suckled him.

His hands grabbed tighter to my hair, grasped my scalp.

Could his amazing control be slipping?

I suckled him even deeper, licking and nipping, my hands rubbing and squeezing his tight butt, my fingers probing his ass. He moaned and bucked, his hands suddenly grabbing my shoulders and I knew he intended to push me away, to keep control of the situation.

I thought of the cocky grin on his face after he'd brought me to climax the second time and for some reason my competitive nature kicked in. I licked the length of his shaft and followed it with one hand, my fingers squeezing and massaging the entire distance, rubbing the tiny drops of pre-cum from his tip to his balls.

I drew one of his testicles into my mouth and he groaned, bucking his hips against my hand as I found my own rhythm...gentle pressure on the testicle in my mouth, more pressure with my fingers as I stroked his penis from crown to base.

I knew he fought for control, but I felt the clenching in his groin, sensed the climax in his hesitation, the catch in his breath. He stilled a moment, that last struggle before orgasm. At that moment I penetrated his ass with my finger, clamped gently down on his testicle between my tongue and the roof of my mouth and squeezed his rampant cock between my fingers.

He shouted when he came, an incoherent cry of release that ended on a shuddering sob, a frantic gasp for breath, a harsh burst of laughter.

Long moments later, he rose up on his elbows and grinned at me.

I will always treasure that look—one of shell-shocked satiation.

"My god, woman. Are you trying to kill me?"

I grinned back at him from my position, still kneeling between his legs. He grabbed me, pulled me across his chest and tucked my head just under his chin.

"Who, me? Nah...just didn't want you to get too cocky."

"I'll get as cocky as I want. Give me a minute so I can get cocky again."

I started to say something about him not getting cocky for at least a week, when I realized his erection had never totally faded.

Realized that's what I felt swelling against my belly, long and hard and already gloriously erect.

I raised one eyebrow and stared at him. He shrugged, as sheepish a look as a drop-dead gorgeous, perfectly cocky middle-aged millionaire who knows he's gonna get laid can have. He kissed me, then reached for the pants I'd casually tossed on the floor.

"This time," he said, pulling a foil wrapped packet out of his pocket, "we're going to do things my way."

I rolled off of him and watched while he carefully slipped the condom over his fully erect penis.

"It's about time," I said. Already my muscles were clenching in anticipation, my breasts tingling, the nipples hard and swollen.

I decided I really liked it when Martin wanted to do things his way.

He started slow and as far from my crotch as he could, kissing my mouth with an intensity that belied the fact he's just come all over his leather sofa. I've never been *explored* before, but that's what Martin did, in a most exquisite fashion.

His tongue teased my lips and tangled with my tongue. He kissed his way along the line of my jaw, blowing light puffs into my ear. I scrunched my shoulder up in reaction to his tickling breaths and he laughed.

He began to work his way across my breasts. I got the giggles. Everything was so sensitive! My skin tingled wherever he touched, my nipples puckered and tightened under the soft caress of his lips, and when he kissed my belly I squirmed away in protest.

"No more," I said, laughing and pulling my knees up to my chest. "I can't take anymore."

I really didn't mean it.

Thank goodness, Martin didn't believe me.

He picked me up and carried me out of the room. I had no idea where he was taking me until I was suddenly deposited in the middle of a huge brass bed.

Practically lost in the thick down comforter, I sat up and brushed the hair back from my eyes. Martin was bearing down on me, a pair of expensive neckties in each hand, his condom-clad erection bobbing against his belly.

I scrambled across the bed but he caught me. I was laughing so hard I couldn't even fight him off when he loosely tied my hands and feet to the bedposts.

I glanced at the knots. If I struggled too hard, they'd come untied.

Okay, so I'd struggle just a little bit.

This time he started with my breasts. He suckled first one, then the other, drawing each of my nipples into his mouth, nipping each one in its turn with his teeth, laving the tortured little buds with his tongue. The sensation was overwhelming, the combination of pleasure and pain exquisite.

I tugged lightly at the silk neckties holding me spread across his bed and realized Martin had fulfilled a fantasy I'd not even realized I had.

He sat back on his heels and smiled at me. I wondered if he was thinking of the dreams, the fact we'd never consummated the sexual act in any of the fantasies.

"You're mine, you know. No woman invades my nights, hell, even my waking hours, with the kind of sensual assault as you have and gets away from me."

"Do you have any idea what happened?" I tugged lightly at the neckties, praying the knots would hold.

Martin shook his head. "Haven't got a clue. But I know what's going to happen next."

He was big and thick and hot and he fit as if I'd been designed exactly for his cock. He filled me, moving slow enough to drive me mad until I arched my back, pressed my hips against his and took him completely inside.

He closed his eyes a moment, then leaned close and began to move, his sheathed penis sliding easily within me. I wanted to wrap my arms around him. Hell, I wanted to wrap my legs around him, too, but the silken ties held me spread out and helpless.

I've never enjoyed helpless so much in my life. Martin found the perfect angle, thrusting in and out of me so that he dragged his cock across my slick clitoris with each stroke. I wanted this to last, wanted to watch him come while I was still in control but the sensations were too much, the pleasure too intense.

I concentrated on the sounds, the soft sucking noise as he withdrew, the gentle slap of his balls against my ass with each forward thrust. I was doing just great until he leaned over and dragged his teeth across my left nipple, suckled it into his mouth and bit down.

I felt the jolt all the way from breast to crotch. Every cliché from every romance I'd ever read popped into mind and just as quickly popped out again.

Gasping, crying, clutching at the neckties holding me captive, I shuddered and screamed out my release.

Still Martin pounded into me. *Too much,* I thought. *It's too much.* Then I felt that familiar coil of desire, that deep clenching that starts in your belly and centers itself in your clit and I went over the top again.

This time Martin went with me.

Eyes closed, cords in his neck straining, the muscles in his powerful arms bulging, he completely lost the cool, urbane control I thought of as his trademark. Lost it with a rasping cry of release, a harsh shout that curled my toes with pure, unadulterated pleasure.

Pleasure and a sense of power, to know I could command him such.

I easily slipped my hands free of their bonds and wrapped my arms around my lover's back. He nuzzled his beard-roughened chin against my collarbone and sighed.

"Will any of this ever make sense?" he mumbled.

"Probably not," I said, barely able to form the words around the broad grin on my face.

"Delgado had me thrown into an empty storage room when they turned off Melinda's air. I found something on the floor. I think it belongs to you. It's in my pants' pocket."

Curiosity consumed me as he pushed himself up and left the room. I quickly untied the neckties and was sitting in the middle of the bed when Martin returned.

He held out his hand, that beautiful, long fingered hand that made my body sing. Lying in his palm was my missing diamond stud.

Chapter Three
ॐ

Hunches are one thing, but what happened between Melinda and me was something else altogether. There's a bond between us that's stronger than the bond most mothers and daughters share.

There's a special bond between Martin and me, too, though the dreams have ended. Even the hot flashes aren't as bad, but that could be the result of an active sex life. I'm convinced getting laid on a regular basis cures most of anyone's ills.

It's done wonders for mine.

I don't miss the dreams because I have Martin, but I'm not sure about the marriage thing. He's very insistent and I can't imagine life without him after this. Maybe some day. My sixth sense tells me I haven't got much choice in the matter, but I'm not willing to capitulate so easily.

Martin can be such a control freak.

It's an especially attractive personality trait in the bedroom.

We never did figure out how my diamond stud ended up in Delgado's quiet room. A room padded and sound-proofed, designed for holding prisoners. I told Martin the first time I noticed it missing was the day we rescued Melinda.

The day I took him in my mouth, first in fantasy, then in reality.

Some questions just don't have easy answers.

At least Martin and Melinda are safe. The bales I hid behind held enough cocaine to put Delgado and his crew behind bars for a long, long time, and kidnapping's always been a capital offense.

I still find myself drifting off in thought, remembering that night as if I'd watched it happening to a lousy actress in a B movie.

When I think of what came later, my first real night with Martin, it's more like a fantasy, a Twentieth Century Fox big screen spectacular. The most wonderful movie I've ever seen in my life and I get to play it over and over and over.

There will always be questions without answers. I left out a lot of details during the investigation and told the DA an old-fashioned reporter's hunch led me to Melinda's prison, a hunch and some things I overheard Delgado say.

Martin's response was a knowing grin, a smile that melted my bones. He didn't mention the dreams we'd once shared, the link that had brought us together in the first place.

He didn't have to.

He did, however, reach up and flick my ear lobe where the diamond stud glittered.

The DA was satisfied with our explanation though, too busy reveling in his newfound role as hero to worry about the details.

It wasn't often, he said, he got the chance to not only kiss two beautiful women in one day, but to have everyone thank him for it.

Melinda was too disoriented at the time to even care how we explained her rescue. At least she accepts me in her father's life without question. She's a busy young woman and she's getting on with her own life, putting as much of this behind her as she can.

One of these days, though, I'm going to ask her just how much she remembers. About me, about the light and the tunnel, and the people gathered there.

One of these days I'll really need to know, really feel a desire to once again get to the bottom of the story, to ferret out the answers, to follow up on my hunches. Then I'll ask Melinda the question that still bedevils my mind.

I wonder if *she* saw Elvis?

Also by Kate Douglas

ക

About the Author

For over thirty years Kate Douglas has been lucky enough to call writing her profession. She has won three EPPIES, two for Best Contemporary Romance and a third for Best Romantic Suspense. She is multi-published in contemporary and paranormal romance, both print and electronic formats, as well as her popular futuristic Romantica™ series, StarQuest. She and her husband of thirty-five years have recently moved to the beautiful mountains of northern California where they find more than enough subject material for their shared passion for photography — though their grandchildren are most often in front of the lens.

Kate welcomes comments from readers. You can find her website and email address on her author bio page at www.ellorascave.com.

Tell Us What You Think

We appreciate hearing reader opinions about our books. You can email us at Comments@EllorasCave.com.

DEATH REBORN
Mari Byrne

∽

Prologue

 හ

The choice is yours. If you wish to step into the role of Death, you may.

The Ascendant's voice drifted through his conscience as it explained that the decision to become Death was his, and his alone. If for any reason the laws were violated, he would suffer the consequences. It was more than could be expected, and much less than he could ever want.

Originally it was the blow of an ancient weapons' devastating impact ending his reality that had sent him to his demise. There had been pain, then nothing but peace. When the peace began to bore him, and thoughts of bargaining for the role of Death and its small privileges were presented, he made the decision to take it.

"I accept."

Waiting for what felt like an eternity, the answer came to him as a mind-blowing shock. The pain was unbearable. Foolishly, he had thought that after death, nothing could ever hurt again.

It hadn't taken long before he discovered just how wrong he was.

* * * * *

That had been his first experience as Death, and he'd never regretted taking up the mantle, until now.

The only thing he wanted at this moment was to give it all up. Break his contract with the Ascendant, and claim the woman he'd waited to claim these last twenty years.

And now he had a plan, a plan for a real life. Remembering it now, Death had to wonder at the calm he'd felt as he and the Ascendant spoke of this bargain.

If she accepts you for who you are, your contract with me shall be broken. The Ascendant's voice boomed around him as he calmly nodded his head. The only thing required of Death to seal the bargain had been his willingness to forsake what he couldn't remember having.

His soul.

His thoughts flew about him as he anticipated seeing her once again, this time as a Man. Knowing it was too much to hope that she would instantly recognize the reason for this particular visit, he nonetheless went about working out the details for their upcoming reunion.

His thoughts were interrupted as he suddenly felt a little one's soul ready to depart. Face and mind blanked, he went about escorting the innocent home.

Chapter One

ɕᴑ

Tawny backed further into the corner, slid down the wall in a crouch and waited for Death to find her. This was the safest place she could think of to hide from him. She wasn't ready to go and would try her damnedest to thwart him. Shit, if he found her — well, she would think of something to negotiate with him for more time.

She had seen Death appear as she made her way down the hall toward the laundry room, arms laden with the last load she had put off doing the night before. She immediately recognized him, or did she?

Trying her best to still her breathing, Tawny willed her mind to think clearly, closing her eyes a moment and tried to bring forward the vision she had of Death from her childhood. In comparing it with the one she'd just seen, Tawny opened her eyes as a frown began to form.

Death he might be, although neither time had she seen him in a long flowing black robe, faceless holding a sickle. In fact, the first time she had *seen* him had been more of a peripheral viewing; she hadn't actually seen clothing, a face or body, just an impression.

This time, she had seen him as if he were real rather than an image. He was flesh and blood in typical male clothing of faded blue jeans, a white, buttoned down shirt with the sleeves rolled up and sneakers. Not clothing she had expected to see when she met Death again for the last time.

Now she began to doubt herself. Making a wry face, she wondered if she had mistakenly marked one of her building's male tenants as Her Nana's Grim Reaper. Feeling slightly foolish, she imagined the man running in the opposite direction for his apartment and the phone.

She chuckled softly as she imagined his end of a conversation with one of his pals.

"I swear! The woman took off as if I was the boogieman, and all I was doing was practicing for my latest reappearing act for my next tour. I'm a magician, it's what I do!"

Tawny shook her head at her silliness and started to dismiss who and what she had seen as that of possibly a magician, a visiting—she groped for a logical explanation of someone who had looked remarkably close to her memory of Death, but who was actually *not* Death.

Her ears straining to hear the slightest sound, she wondered if she should get up, admit she was being fanciful and go finish her laundry. Praying silently that her movements made no sound, because deep down she thought *what if it really had been him*, she began turning her head. Suddenly she gasped in shock as she found a man's silhouette before her on the folding screen.

Unintentionally having given away her hiding place, she watched now as his hand reached out, pushing aside the flimsy barrier she had hastily thought could keep someone at bay. Still crouching, she starred gapingly up at him, any previous thoughts of whether he was Death or not fleeing her mind.

If this man was Death then there were very few arguments she would use against following him to her demise.

God! The man was temptation incarnate!

Long lashed, sensual, midnight blue eyes locked with her suddenly fascinated green eyes and pierced into her soul, leaving her with feelings that had everything to do with *lé petite mort* and little with the "may she forever rest in peace".

She found herself eagerly wanting to embrace him, to discover exactly what feelings his eyes spoke of. Eyes that seemed to look at her with craving hunger and burning sensuality, while soothing away any fear she'd experienced upon his abrupt appearance.

Her body sprang instantaneously to life, and began adjusting itself to his presence, readying itself in an internal dance of sensuality as old as time itself.

His coal black hair seemed made for her fingers to run through its' silky length. His hair surrounded a thin, angular face, with sculptured high cheekbones and an aquiline nose. A thin upper lip that hung over a lush bottom one that begged a woman to bite into it and then suck gently to soothe. He also possessed a square, strong chin that spoke of the strength you would find in him.

She could see muscles rippling that hinted at the strength his body held even as she was compelled by an ingrained desire to grab hold of him and ride that body all night long. Longing and a pull so violent she could not refuse it, ran through her body to devour the rippling muscled offering before her.

The air of suppressed hunger coming off him, all but left her breathless, lightheaded from desire, and weak with a lust she had never before craved. His body had to have been a gift from God.

He held out his hand to her, she swallowed hard and waited for him to speak.

"It's time."

In spite of the fear running through her, something deep inside Tawny clenched in violent hunger at the sound of his deep sensuous voice. Her sudden want of the man made her gasp, and her mind wonder at its' abrupt change toward the man. Looking from his outstretched hand, to his granite face, and finding a look of carnal hunger in his dark eyes, her mind shut off all previous thoughts of running from him.

This man was going to eat her alive, she realized as her pussy began to spill wet heat and her nipples pinched into aching beads that longed to have his mouth soothe them. Her eyes closed as overwhelming emotions rolled over and through her.

The breath Tawny had been holding whooshed out as she immersed herself in the emotions Death brought out of her. She acknowledged there was a feeling of his being very important to her life and its' goals.

I am willingly...No eagerly, going to give myself to this man, and damning whatever consequences come from my actions. Something in my soul is answering the demand that I completely give myself over to him. A pull so strong that even at death, I cannot deny. My choice has been made.

* * * * *

His nostrils flared as he inhaled the mixture of fear and excitement coming from his woman. Hearing her attempts to still her breath made his cock shift in hunger and his blood flow faster. Reaching down, he adjusted the weight of his stiff rod and tried to hold back the image of thrusting into Tawny until he spent himself dry. His ultimate goal was for her to gain satisfaction, and it would be his mission, and his alone, to give her that satisfaction.

His other goal would take a little more concentration than he had at the moment, so he pushed it to the back of his mind and concentrated his attention instead on Tawny.

His thoughts were linked clearly with hers and he knew the moment she recognized him and had run. Her mind had passed one thought to her feet, that Death was here for her, and she had bolted thinking to escape him. He chuckled at the thought, and with a possessive smile, had gone after her.

He'd paused silently at the end of the corridor and inhaled to follow her scent. Turning left, he'd found the room she was in just off to the right side where a hidden doorway lay sunk into the wall as if it was merely another groove where the paneling met. His unique senses had told him that that was where he would find her, just as the tangy smell emanating from her let him know unequivocally that her body was readying itself for him and his seduction.

Moving forward on silent feet, he'd reached the hidden door, and used every skill learned as Death to open it soundlessly. Stepping through the doorway, finding nothing with his eyes, he shut them and used his other senses as a guide.

Successfully finding her this way, he'd discarded the barrier she was behind, stood before her and waited silently. It hadn't taken long for her eyes to open and skim their way up his body until they'd met his.

"It's time."

Using only those two words, Death now looked down at Tawny and waited for her to take his hand before beginning his assault on her senses.

He could feel the hunger running through her body as if it was his own. Feeling as if he had hungered an eternity for her, now that she was within his reach, nothing would stop him from having her.

He'd first seen her at the age of eleven, when the time had come to collect her Nana's soul. As he'd entered her Grandma's room and sat down next to her Nana, Tawny had seen his facade, ignored it, and gone back to calmly telling the woman she had adored so much in life, good-bye.

He'd waited patiently for Tawny to finish her farewell to her Nana, and in the watching, had become fascinated with her. She'd spoken as if much older than her chronological age, and something in him opened, unfurling from somewhere deep inside his soul, which had been deeply buried under years of negativity.

In the time it had taken her to finish her farewell, he fell heavily under a spell her voice had woven around his emotions. It'd taken precious little time for him to realize she was the *one*.

His soul mate.

It'd taken all he had left in him not to leave the older woman's soul, and instead snatch her Granddaughter's and run with it to some place no one or thing, could ever find them. Instead, he'd dipped his head in an acknowledging nod to the young Tawny, gripped her Nana's hand in his, and walked the old woman's soul toward her final reward. Before they'd slipped away completely, he heard Tawny speak.

"Nana said you would soon come back for me." She'd made the statement, and all Death could do was nod his head as he'd made the girl's heart a promise, while Tawny watched he and her Nana, disappear.

Now, bending a little more toward her, he waited until she finally took his offered hand, helped her stand, and tucked her protectively into his body. For a moment neither moved. For him it was because she was finally in his arms. Reading her thoughts easily, he found that for her, it was because she always wanted to remember the final moment of her life.

Feeling her shiver, he wanted to ease her fears. As intoxicating and heady as the sensation was to him, fear was the last sensation he wanted her to feel at this moment.

"Relax," he whispered into her ear. "I am not here for the reason you believe." The last words trailed away as he opened his mouth and bending his head, tasted her skin.

Chapter Two
❧

Relaxing her hands out of their tightly clinched fists, she steadied herself by grasping her hands around his muscled arms. His mouth moved to the bend in her neck, and he began to nibble and suckle lightly on one of the most sensitive areas of her body.

She knew she was in deep when her panties dampened with no more than a tiny bite and suck. Turning her head to look at him, Tawny found lust-filled eyes open and staring at her.

"Do you remember who I am?" she heard him ask even as his hands continued their exploration.

Her memory of him was vivid. Even at so young an age, her feelings toward him had been strong. Her younger self had felt possessive with a certainty that both his soul and hers belonged together. Later the feeling that each of them always seemed to miss each opportunity they had been given to be with each other. Some cruel act of fate, time, or circumstance had blocked their paths.

Now, no obstacle would stand in the way of their being together for this short time.

Whilst slowly nodding her head and staring into those eyes, Tawny watched, as color seemed to bleed into them as he played her body like a fine tuned instrument. His eyes darkened until she was feeling exactly what she saw being played out in his eyes.

Lightening darts of pleasure stabbed at her core as he plucked at a nipple. Her body ached as creamy moisture leaked from her pussy, the longing to be filled with his cock running through her, and the aching need for satisfaction she now knew would only be found with him.

"Why—uhhh!" She tried to ask a question, but her thoughts trailed away when he placed his finger over her open mouth and made a shushing noise.

"I have come to claim what is mine." His husky, gravely reply came as he read her thoughts. "Do you understand?" He breathed.

Closing her eyes momentarily, Tawny gave a nod and opened her eyes to look once more into his.

She found a look in his eyes that told her she wasn't the only one who ached with unfulfilled lust. Looking closer, she saw his own desire leap through his eyes, as his nostrils seemed to flare in response to every drop her aching loins spilled. She watched his mouth open slightly allowing her to hear his strained breathing and her eyes darted down to his lush lips as his tongue darted out to lick at his lips as if she were a tasty morsel he was preparing to devour.

Seeing his eyes grow completely black, the irises bleeding into solid obsidian, her heart began to race as a tiny frisson of her newly found womanly power flowed through her body.

She wanted to be devoured by his frenzied passion, needing him to assuage the yearning he'd created that was, even now riding her loins like a raging bull. The ache and craving for him flowed through every inch of her body, and she would let nothing stop him from alleviating her suffering through an orgasm.

It sounded greedy, and it was. She didn't care. Soon they would both get what they wanted.

"Yes."

It was all that was needed. She would wonder later if her words were said out loud, or if her need of the moment was so great that he heard it from her body instead.

Her eyes closed once again as flames leapt through his eyes into hers and burned a trail into her brain shattering all thoughts but those of heat and desire running between them both.

Her skin tasted of salt and the chemicals used in soaps and lotions. He was finding he could barely taste *her* under all the other flavors. He longed to get them both to a water source where it could all be washed away and he would be able to taste her real flavor. And he would, right after they took the edge off their straining libidos.

Turning her in his arms and resting her back against the surface of the wall, he tried to look into her eyes. When she continued to keep her eyes closed, he put a finger under her chin and gently lifted her head to look at him, wanting to make absolute sure that all her fear was gone.

"Open your eyes. I want to see *you*." He waited for her to comply, and when she did, the power of lust in her eyes hit him like a physical blow. His cock ached unbearably, driving his need to mate immediately with this woman. He must have her or live eternally with the pain of unfulfilled desire.

Even at his death, there hadn't been this much pain driving him to escape into a world of pleasure.

Now looking into her eyes, watching as her pupils dilate, he found her sultry orbs crying frustrated tears for him to ease the ache that thundered and crashed through her veins.

Holding Tawny closer, he found her body, mind, and conscious were all in agreement. Her eyes closed briefly, then opened for him to see the longing he knew was mirrored in his own eyes.

His cock twitched in answer at the thoughts his mind was having of the things he was going to do to her. Needing her to accept all he was going to give her, his voice came out sounding like ground gravel.

"Stand just where you are." Death growled as his hand moved down to unbutton her shirt. "No, don't move," he rasped again when she would have reached out for him. "I want to pleasure you, and to do that, you must keep your hands to yourself."

He could have made her submit to his will, but it was very important to him that she comply with the man he was now trying to be, rather than the Power he had previously chosen.

When Tawny's body stilled, he continued undressing her. Not fully, as he wasn't ready for that yet. For now, he was going to explore her lush figure and remember just what it was to hold and stroke a woman.

Managing all of her buttons and tugging at the shirt to get it out of her jeans, Death tried to still the beast in him that wanted to just rip the clothes off and get to the woman. No, first he was going to make her slippery wet, and so eager for him to slam his cock into her pussy that all she would be able to do was beg him to make her come.

It mostly worked, but when his skin touched hers, Death looked down to find he still held a torn piece of clothing in his clenched fist. He rumbled an apology, spread his fingers wide over her soft belly and let the piece fall from his hand. The feel of her skin under his palms was that of the finest silk it had been his privilege to touch.

In his universe, he rarely touched people. He laid Death's hand on them, but that was all. There was no skin to skin in the touch he gave, only hand to soul; or very rarely, hand to nothing.

Tawny continued to hold still, and Lucas silently thanked her for it. If she moved at this point, his beast might think it was denial and he shuddered at what could happen.

Pushing those thoughts and the consequences from his mind, he ran the tips of his fingers over the swells of her breasts and marveled at God's creation of woman. *He* was ingenious, and should be praised for this wonderful achievement alone.

Death bent his head and used his tongue to take a quick taste of her skin finding the taste of the top swell of her breasts was much closer to her own flavor than it was on her neck. Reveling in it for a moment, he let his hands wander around to her back, dipping lower, learning her with his fingertips as well as with his mouth, and finding that she could no more stand still under his hands than he could stop himself from taking her.

His hands made their way down to the swell of her hips, moved to clutch them under her ass where he kneaded them gently as he ground his cock against her mound. The feel of the heat coming off the juncture of her thighs had him grunting out his pleasure as she tentatively pressed back against him.

To keep from ending the torment too soon, he changed the direction of his seeking hands and ran them lightly back up her body. Slipping them under the loose edges of her shirt, her bra immediately became a barrier. He began ripping at the cloths, tearing them so they slid down her body to land at their feet.

Straightening slightly to take in the view of his bounty, he found two satiny globes of silky flesh that shimmied while she trembled. The sight made him want to sink his teeth into her breasts just to have the pleasure of soothing them with his mouth and tongue.

With rapidly retreating will power, he barely restrained himself when he looked to her face, and found she was watching everything he was doing. It excited him as nothing else did, and his growls continued unabated. Feeling like an animal claiming its mate, he closed his eyes and shook his head slightly to clear out his head and search for a little better control. When he again looked into her eyes, he found he could manage.

When she would have spoken, he touched his finger to her mouth, giving a negative shake of his head. Keeping his eyes on her, he slowly unbuttoned his own shirt and tugged its' shirt tales from his jeans. Spreading the edges wide took a step closer and leaned his upper torso into hers rubbing his chest against her pebbled breasts and found the contact alone was erotic.

She reached up wrapping her arms around him, as he leaned down and took her mouth with frantic need, swirling and stabbing his tongue along and around her tongue, mimicking the thrusting his cock would soon repeat in her wet heat. She met his invasion with a healthy dose of her own need beginning to make itself known in the kiss.

Yes, the thought ran through him, *this I remember*!

The touch of man to woman, the feel of being nipple to nipple, groin to groin. The remembered pleasure of sliding his cock into a warm wet woman and bringing her to a frenzied, fiery, screaming release. Tongues dueling for pleasure together rather than spouting words of hate or regret. The memory of his dick being squeezed unbelievably tight while a woman came in rivers and drowned his cock in pleasure.

This time, the memory would be doubly pleasing as he now had the opportunity to fuck his chosen mate. He sent a silent plea to *Him* praying he would never again forget this feeling.

Narrowing his focus down to his woman, he inserted a knee between her legs, tucked his thigh tightly upward, and left her to straddle his leg. He used his hands to stroke the parts of her body that weren't already covered by him.

Moving his hands to her hips, he started sawing her mons back and forth against his thigh. Despite their jeans he could still feel the heat and wetness he was causing her pussy to emote, triggering his cock to stretch even further.

Knowing he should object when Tawny started to move, his mind instead strayed to the goal he had in his sights.

Her pleasure. Right now, he wasn't in the mood to give up the pleasure he would get from her when she came.

Tawny barely noticed when her hips began to rock against his thigh of their own accord. All of her concentration was focused on the effects he was having on her body. She had heard the growl come from him, and it turned her on even more causing her hips to grind down harder against his thigh.

She was floating adrift on a sensual haze. It took her a few moments to realize he had slowed his motions and was looking at her again. Her body had been moving to the rhythms his hands set in motion without any prompting from her mind. His hungry movements had carried her along with him and she had reveled in them.

She opened her eyes fully, her body now on fire, and found that the hungry look of earlier had metamorphosed into looks of complete and utter starvation, stunned longing, insatiable hunger and something indefinable.

It was a look that said he really *was* going to eat her all up and she was going to love every minute of it.

Tawny watched Death as his eyes closed tightly and he sucked in his breath deeply. The sight of this tightly controlled man coming close to losing himself over her turned her on more than anything she had ever seen or done. When he seemed to have himself in hand, he opened his eyes and looked down at where his leg met her body.

He dropped his leg slightly allowing her to touch tiptoes on the floor while making some room between them where none had been before.

She made a sound somewhere between frustration and acute physical pain, and closed her eyes to take away the visual temptation in front of her but found it didn't help. Opening her eyes, Tawny looked down and knew the only thing to be of any help in her current situation would be what he hid from her with his pants.

Death watched as Tawny stood on tiptoe and waited for her eyes to refocus on him. When at last they did, he saw her look at his face, then down toward the hard-on pressing ever forward in an effort to escape his pants. His rigidly held control snapped, her excitement was too much, and grasping both sides of her jeans, he tore them off in two almost cleanly ripped halves.

He quickly looked to her for her reaction. But all Tawny did was look at her torn clothing and give a relieved sigh. In a voice made husky from unfulfilled desire, he heard her grate out, "I was wondering how they were going to come off without you moving away from me."

He sensed the change in her from earlier. She reached out and grasped one of the halves in her hand, carelessly tossing it to the side.

"Shall we continue?"

Growling deep in his chest, Death dropped to his knees and reached out hands that shook slightly to bring her body closer to him. Grasping her around her satiny thighs, he propelled her forward even as he lifted his head up to look at her, and spoke.

"I don't want to frighten you, but please, don't deny me." He could have explained, but was past the point of speaking much more, and for the moment she didn't seem to care.

"Deny you?" Tawny asked hoarsely. "Not in this lifetime, or the next!"

Feeling dainty cloth in front of his mouth, Death gave a slightly devilish laugh thinking the tiny scrap didn't stand a chance against him. Leaning in closer he grasped the fabric gently between his teeth, scraping her sensitive mons lightly with his teeth. Giving a tug of the fabric and humming joyfully as it succumbed, he revealed her.

Leaning back, he stared at part of the prize he had bargained with the Ascendant for and found he wanted to savor the exquisite sight further.

Her woman's lips pouted and twitched as he reached out a finger and traced one side from the outside tip to where it turned to fold inward. He heard a tiny indrawn breath as he followed the line further inward and dipped the single digit into the hot juice pooling and escaping. He brought the finger up to his nostril, inhaling deeply, making his head spin at the piquant bouquet.

He looked upward to find her eyes rounded in surprised wonder. Moving his finger to his mouth, his tongue darted to his finger to taste her essence. The flavor to him was ambrosia; a taste denied mortals, but left for the gods to feast on. It was all he could do not to open his mouth wide and swallow this treasure before him whole.

But that wasn't what he was here for, at least not yet. Instead of devouring her whole, he was here to fulfill his promise of coming back for her, and staking his claim for his soul mate.

Now, remembering the deal he made with himself to give pleasure to this woman, and to receive it in return, was all he could think about while so close to Tawny. He wouldn't go back on it for anything.

A frenzied smile suddenly showed on his lips as her scent began to entice him in closer. At the last minute, when he would have plunged full ahead, he denied himself and instead turned his mouth into the juncture where thigh met torso. He thrust out his tongue, laving at the bend, and found the flavor here much closer to her natural scent, an intoxicating blend of Tawny and nature. Her potent combination was enough to once again make him feel like a whole man.

Making his way over to her nest of curls that tickled his cheek, he used his lips to worry around the edges of her crease. Hearing her muted pleas, his throbbing cock jumped at each and every one as he finally turned to nuzzle the springy hair aside with his tongue and find the tender skin beneath.

Using his tongue to explore her opening, he ran it from top to bottom while he brought up his hands to cup her buttocks. Once there, he kneaded her cheeks while gripping and clenching them in turn.

His tongue plunged further into her curls and found to his delight her tiny beaded pearl. Moving his hands, he spread her legs further apart, swirled the little bead into his mouth and began suckling it gently.

Tawny stared down at the top of Death's head. The sight of him between her legs sent another gush of cream out of her already drenched pussy, immediately followed by the feeling of his tongue lapping faster and his mouth increasing suction on her clit.

Tawny tried to draw breath enough to scream out at the sensations invading her lower body as he used his tongue in devastating pleasure, but he had effectively taken normal breathing capabilities from her. All she could do at this point was hold on, wallowing in the mind-blowing sensations he brought out of her, and hope he didn't drown in her desire.

He could feel her legs begin to buckle and immediately rearranged them both so she now straddled his shoulders, using the wall to lean back on. This opened her even further, and to his delight, he found better access to the gem he was greedily devouring.

With skilled hands, he managed to continue his massage of her tender buttocks at the same time using a thumb to open her pussy. He stopped suckling her clit long enough to look down and find Tawny completely open to him. It fascinated him to watch his thumb plunge in and out of her pussy. Bending his head once more, he alternated between nibbling at her clitoris and using his tongue to consume her very essence.

Teetering on the brink, so close to orgasm, Tawny finally began thrusting her hips greedily forward until the feeling of being impaled by Death's teeth and tongue became the only sensations of her universe. Death made his final assault on her cunt. He thrust his tongue deep once, twice…and that's all it took. She came apart in his arms. Screaming, she rode through the mind shattering, body twitching, blissful moment as Death continued eating at her.

Tawny had no concept of how long she lay back against the wall panting, but found when she came to herself once more, Death's tongue still lapped lightly, licking at her core. She briefly tried scooting away, but his hold remained firm. Almost immediately, Tawny gave up any attempt to evade his reach, surrendering herself to him instead.

Grasping onto his hair, she poised herself for another wild ride while the continued movements of his laving tongue sent her already aroused body into another explosion of pleasure. Death kept this orgasm riding hard.

When it finally subsided into soft contractions, Death lifted his head to speak.

"More." His beast spoke for him as they both yearned to devour the woman who gave herself so freely.

Sated for the moment, Tawny felt a sense of peace invade her soul. Looking at Death, an inexplicable feeling came over her. The sense of peace, this wholeness she felt, had come with the man before her.

Chapter Three

ɛ૭

Death handed his shirt over to Tawny. "Here, put this on," he said in a terse voice laced heavily with need. Covered now, he bent, picked Tawny up in his arms, and quickly strode to the door. Finding the handle to open it, he gave what he thought was a gentle tug, and instead ripped the door from its hinges. Snarling at it, he flung it aside, telling himself he would see it fixed later.

He went through the door turning left, his stride eating up the distance to the elevator where he jammed his thumb onto the button and held it while waiting for the car to arrive. He used his incredible strength to hold onto Tawny who lay sprawled in his other arm, then let up on the button momentarily to stroke his finger down her cheek, before stabbing once more at the up button.

When the car finally arrived, he stepped into it, slammed a fist at the button for Tawny's floor, while suppressing an impatient growl, stood waiting for the elevator to fling them both upward. He looked down at Tawny, unable to help himself and crushed her slack mouth with his hungry lips.

He devoured her mouth like a man starving, and Tawny stirred, beginning to squirm in his arms. Both so intent on each other they ceased to notice the elevator finally reaching her floor.

An older couple standing in the open doorway stared in amazed shock as Death lifted his head, turned and looked at them. The woman was the first to regain her composure. Her stunned look turning into a knowing smile instead.

"George," she turned toward her husband nudging his arm none too gently. "I've changed my mind. Bingo can wait, we're staying in tonight!" Turning her head to look at Death and Tawny, she gave them a saucy wink, and she dragged her husband back the way they had come.

Death chuckled huskily as he moved toward Tawny's door. Looking down at her, he did his best to bank the hunger raging through him. She was a bountiful feast for a starving demon, and he would fill himself to bursting with her before they were through this long day.

Flicking his fingers outward, too impatient and aroused to be bothered using mortal means to achieve his wants, the door opened under his will power. Walking through the entrance, not stopping until he reached the decadent bathroom he had sensed in her home. Again, he flicked a finger, the water in the shower turned on in a raging torrent that sent steam billowing over the top of the stall's door.

Looking down at Tawny still held in his arms, he barely resisted standing her against the wall and ramming himself into her still slick, wet, and very hot, passage. The only thing stopping him now was the promise he made himself to cleanse her thoroughly and taste her every inch at his leisure.

Setting Tawny in the shower and hurriedly stripping, he barely waited for her to steady herself against the wall, before calling up the purification oil he used for himself. It was time to cleanse every nook and cranny he could find and when he was finished, he was going to fully indulge himself, with her.

Stepping into the shower behind her while keeping hold of her hand, Death shut the glass door then turned her body to face him. Her eyes were closed to keep the water out and the picture she made standing under the water's spray sent his already rampant cock swelling larger.

He wanted to lick away every drop of water from her body in long, slow, tormenting strokes, and when she thought she couldn't take another second more, he'd do it again.

He seemed to be getting ahead of himself. Right now, he was going to wash away anything that would mar the taste of her natural quintessence. Reaching out and touching the oil to her neck, he proceeded to learn every inch of her body, leaving no area untouched.

Death sensed just how close she was to another release and feelings of intense male pride ran through him. He had wanted to wait until they were horizontal, but realized that was not going to happen this time either.

With a fierce growl issuing from his throat, he turned his attention to seeing that the lady got what she needed.

Tawny stood in the shower letting the water pulse down her body and wondered just what was going through his mind. She had seen the door open and close by itself as he had stalked through her home, coming to stand in her spacious bathroom.

It was true. All things bowed to his will, including inanimate objects. He had control over all he saw and touched, and she wondered why she was still here. Instead of bringing her a true death, his magical hands and mouth had brought her body to glorious life and she would never be the same again.

Intending to clean up, she thoroughly wet her hair. But when she would have reached for the shampoo, his large hands reached out grasping onto her, and stopped her motion.

"No, " the word coming out rough, almost harsh. "I will give you everything you need tonight." He proceeded to wash her as if needing to learn all the secrets of her body.

Tawny couldn't help herself. She began withering and bucking at his slightest touch on her body. The feeling of his nimble hands upon her already inflamed form, ignited fires she pleaded for him to extinguish.

Her body was one large erogenous zone that he mapped, both front and back, using his hands, teeth, and tongue. One hand moved across her breast as his fingers paid homage to her puckered nipples. His other hand snaked down her body delving into her thatch to strum her clit with his thumb and ream her ass with his finger.

She could only stand in place, moaning out yet another plea, begging him to let her come now, Now, NOW!

Barely aware of the water going off as Death positioned her to face the wall of the shower, Tawny could only comply with his wants. He gently pressed the side of her face against the tile wall with his own, his body spooning hers.

*Death...*Her thoughts of gaining satisfaction momentarily paused. At some other time he must have gone by another name, there had to be something else she could call him instead of Death. The feelings he was arousing in her no way inspired thoughts of a state of not living.

"Please—" she implored him. It came out breathy and needy. She cleared her throat softly before trying again. "Please. Tell me—"

She really did try to ask, but suddenly, his hands slipped under her arms placing them high on the shower wall. He slid them down and around, while he grasped hold of her nipples, rolling them between his fingers and interspersing his action with gentle squeezes. The exquisite feeling began a deep burning in her core as he used the edge of his nail in a contrasting way to scrape gently against her nipples, breathing sound into her ear.

"Lucas."

The name sent a frisson of pleasure coursing through her. His thick, raspy, voice, his incredibly adept hands, and his hard cock presently nudging against her ass cheeks, all made her cunt flow freely with creamy juices. Lucas bent his legs and repositioned his cock to nudge her pussy's entrance.

Tawny could barely keep her arms up as Lucas enveloped her.

Lucas continued using his fingers to massage her clit while he rocked his hips back and forth to tease his cock into her cunt.

He pinched his fingers against her clit the same way he had used his tongue earlier, with devastating expertise causing Tawny to squirm and twist her body in an attempt to impale herself on his hot pulsating cock. No matter what she tried, Lucas held her in place and continued to rock himself back and forth against her slick, heated cunt.

He squeezed his eyes closed and tried to think of anything else but the fact that he was finally going to bury himself in the only woman he had ever wanted to risk his eternal soul for, but nothing worked. Wherever he looked for a distraction, nothing allowed him to forget that he had his cock between the legs of the woman he had hungered so long for.

Now, with her hot, tight pussy sucking rhythmically at his cock while her body pulsed in pleasure, Lucas's rigid control on his own lust snapped.

He pulled his cock almost completely away from her sheath, barely waiting for Tawny to adjust her step and plant her feet, before he sank fully into her, burying his cock to the hilt.

He tried to keep the pace slow when he finally began to slide in and out of her creamy heated depths, but found it impossible.

He heard her begging plead for completion escape and bracing his hands on her waist, began to thrust faster and faster until her cunt begin to contract around him.

The sound of his name being shouted when she came drew his own surrender out of him. Losing the battle with his steely control he began pistoning his hips, slamming his cock in and out. His own release broke over him, and shuddering in pleasure his cock pumped stream after stream of hot fluid into her cunt.

He might have actually left his mortal body, but couldn't be absolutely sure. Right now he couldn't be sure of anything. His muscles felt like liquefied jelly that had been left in the sun too long, and he didn't want to move. Tawny had other ideas though as he heard her breathing catch when he tried to move to a more comfortable position.

Chuckling softly, he slipped out of her. Changing their positions by wrapping her arms and legs around his back, he used his muscled arms to embrace her, securing her with his hands on her ass. This also allowed him to slip his still hard cock back into her pussy startling a short, surprised, gasp of delight out of her.

The gasp immediately turned into simultaneous groans of longing as he began the process of getting them out of the shower.

Carrying her in this position teased him as much as her, and snagging a towel off her sink, they headed straight through to her living room. He began imagining all of the things he still wanted to do to her, thinking how he couldn't get enough of her, didn't even want to leave her body for the little time it would take to get them both dry.

One orgasm with this woman would never suffice. Hell, a lifetime of loving this woman wouldn't be enough for him. He had every intention of trying to make up for it all day and night long. This time might have to serve him as all he would ever have of her.

There was no guarantee his plan would work.

However, his plan for using his still rock hard cock, hands, and mouth on her extremely responsive body over and over through the night and into the next morning, was still first priority.

Bending his head toward her now, he took her lips and mouth with his trying to convey all his thanks, pleasure, wants, hopes and dreams in one blazing moment.

Lucas's mouth brushed her lips, and Tawny sighed at the sensory pleasure. When he brushed her mouth a second time, Tawny noticed immediately the intensity of his kiss changed.

He began eating at her mouth with his teeth and tongue as if he couldn't get enough of her. Shivering slightly, her body and hair still damp, she returned his kiss with all the longing inside her for the man he was.

He was heat and ice all rolled into one and gave her body the most delicious chills as he took her mouth in a soul-searing kiss. Her heart skipped a beat while feelings of lust, and surprisingly enough love, broke over her. His cock expanded filling her core and she began the erotic climb once more as he walked.

When they finally broke the kiss, she was breathing hard from more than just lack of oxygen. He had quite effectively forged her body's reactions back into an almost frenzy. Her body responded to his as if it had already learned the ways to ignite flames to a flash burning point.

Dazed from his kiss and the delicious movements their bodies made, she looked behind her with the intent of orienting herself to her surroundings once again and found he had stopped walking.

They stood before the sliding glass door of her balcony and he reached out with a casual lift of his hand opening the door. Still watching as he held her easily with one hand under her bottom, she saw him use his other hand to alter her tiny patio that hung six floors above street level.

It seemed to expand in size, and instead of the two plastic lounging chairs and small barbecue she'd placed there when moving in, her patio transformed to three times its own size, the floor of it now becoming transparent and beginning to undulate.

Turning her head back to look at him, her eyes wide in wonder, mouth agape, and an unexpected groan of pleasure escaping, she watched a smile playing over his mouth. He quickly looked to her, and gestured with his head and eyes for her to look again.

She angled her body backward, the movement making her eyes close briefly as darting pleasure pierced through her groin. When the sensations quieted, she opened her eyes dreamily and found he had added equipment she had only ever heard about.

One of the girls she worked with had come in one Monday morning and told anyone who would listen about her wild weekend of mind numbing, mind-blowing sex. She'd described, in wicked detail, what had been done to her. Tawny's ears had perked up when she heard the woman describe a jungle gym type of apparatus.

She found herself now looking at what she had seen in her own mind of the description the woman had given for the devise. Tawny had dubbed it the Sex Jungle-Gym and fantasized about someone strapping her to it and having his way with her.

Looking back at Lucas with wonderment in her eyes, she now fantasized about what she could do to *him* on it! Smiling down at her, as though he knew her thoughts, she watched his head shake while he spoke.

"Perhaps next time. Right now," he punctuated the statement with a swivel of his hips that remind her that they weren't quite finished yet, "I want the whole world to watch as I claim you as mine."

With a glimpse of wicked intent on his face, Lucas stepped out onto the newly finished patio clutching Tawny to his chest as he began whispering softly into her ear, describing in intimate detail exactly what he intended to do to her.

All Tawny could do was listen with rapt attention and feel as her body began to make its urgency for release known.

Her heart leapt to exhilarating life against his chest as she bore down on his aching cock. His eyes began to close in rapturous pleasure, but he forced them open quickly, not wanting to miss even a moment of her pleasure.

Easily balancing them both, he continued toward the jungle-gym with every intention of setting Tawny down on the nearest surface and slamming his cock into her cunt until they both screamed their orgasms to the world. He found that the image he had briefly glimpsed crossing through Tawny's mind was more erotic than even he could pass up. Tawny's mouth wrapped around his cock—

No. First, he was going to fuck her hard and fast because there was no way he was going to slip out of her hot cunt right now. Going to his knees on undulating floor, he gently laid her squirming body down without breaking their intimate contact. Her momentary protest as he reared upward to a sitting position was drowned out as he broke the grip she had on his neck.

He moved her legs, positioning them so the back of her thighs lay on his chest, and spread them, slinging one leg over each elbow. This brought him so close to her cunt that when he looked down, he could see their pubic hairs mingling.

The sight of her opened to him like this, opened for the entire world below or above them, to see him sinking every bit of his cock into her as he staked *his* claim, caused the loss of his control once again. Tilting his pelvis into hers bringing them minutely closer, he reached one hand out to stroke the tiny pearl peaking out from between the two swollen lips of her pussy.

Lucas watched Tawny's hips pumping faster and faster in time with the surging motion of the floor, his breath coming hard and fast now as he matched her and the floor's motions with his own hips. Angling his hips, he used short strokes to slide in and out of her as his balls slapped at her ass, and prayed that his climax would wait for hers.

He began lightly pinching and stroking her clit, and when he looked up towards her face, found the most erotic sight.

She had taken her generously endowed breasts in hand and he watched as she alternately kneaded them while pinching at her nipples. The sight of Tawny bringing herself pleasure in this way had him knowing it wouldn't be much longer for his own orgasm to send him on his own trip through nirvana.

"Lucas...*harder!*" The cry broke from her lips and caused his balls to curl even tighter inward against his body. His cock finally took control from his mind, and he began shooting hot jets of creamy come into her.

He vaguely saw the moment Tawny slipped hard over the edge of her orgasm, crying out a litany of pleasure as his body continued to slap into hers in hard awkward jerks as her cunt clamped down around his still erupting cock.

Tawny's body continued to vibrate and quiver through the orgasm that had crashed throughout her body, breaking through just as she felt Lucas's cock jerk as he came.

She laid still now, his heavy weight a comforting blanket as she remembered the eroticism of being fucked where anyone and everyone could see her. When she had first seen the transparent undulating floor, her heart had stuttered at the thought of anyone else seeing them coupling. No sooner had the thought started than she had dismissed it.

I am his now. Forever.

Her pussy had been so wet around his cock it was all she could do not to drop her legs, trip him to the floor, and follow him down. The fact that anyone could see them had added another layer of feeling to her already stimulated body. The thrill was one she had secretly longed for anyway, and she wouldn't have denied either of them a chance to play it out.

Now, lying on the cushiony floor that rocked the two of them slowly as if to cradle their bodies, she remembered exactly what had set her off into a screaming orgasm.

From nowhere, the picture of her kneeling at the feet of Lucas while he stood tall, his cock buried deep in her throat, his hips pumping back and forth toward her face, had sent her plunging into the orgasm. Thinking of it now in the rosy after glow of her bliss, she smiled to herself making a promise to fulfill that dream by morning.

The same thought of swallowing his cock deep, now caused her sated body to initiate its lustful rise once again.

* * * * *

Tawny lay in a slightly arched position, naked, head titled back and her curved body stretched taught. Her arms and legs were tied at four separate points to the jungle-gym, still sitting in the same place it had first appeared.

Lucas stood staring at Tawny, stroking his fully lengthened cock in an absent-minded gesture. He watched as Tawny tried in vain to squirm in the straps he'd used on her wrist and ankles. The best she could do was wiggle her hips minutely as she tested her bonds. The imploring little whimpers she made were the sweetest sounds he'd heard in a millennia.

Moving to stand in front of her titled face, he stooped down, cradling her head while lifting it as he looked down into her hungry eyes.

"I don't know if it will be enough." Tawny blurted out as she looked up into Lucas's eyes. Giving her a quizzical look, Lucas opened his mouth to ask her to explain, but was cut off as she began to speak again.

"Our time together, right now. I don't think it will be enough. I—" She pulled futilely at her bonds, wishing her hands were free to touch him as she told him what lay in her heart.

Giving an impatient growl, she glared at the ties that bond her before turning back to Lucas.

"I love you. I will always—" Tawny words were abruptly cut off when Lucas brought his mouth crashing down onto hers.

When Lucas let them both up for air, Tawny stared up at him, her eyes full with the love she felt for him. She knew suddenly, this *would* be enough, and smiling at him as he stroked her hair, she tried to speak.

"I take it back. It's enough. It's more than I'd hoped for, and I—" Her words trailed away once more as Lucas bent his head and drove all thought out of her mind.

Chapter Four
Before Dawn
ଛ

Tawny awoke to find Lucas watching her wake from a chair opposite the window. Smiling tentatively at him, she turned her head on the pillow, finding a better angle to see him without getting up.

She spoke first as he seemed inclined to remain silent.

"It's almost dawn," she began as her eyes darted toward the window, then back to where he sat. She had made up her mind to confront him, and knew it was now or never.

"How much longer do I have?"

He remained silent, looking at her with a tiny smile on his lips, as if he held a secret closely inside, just waiting for the right time to reveal it.

"I came here with the intention of claiming you. You are all I have thought of for the last twenty years. My soul, when I allowed it, ached to join with yours. The Ascendant and I made a bargain. For me to claim you, I agreed to no longer be Death, but as human as I was before I died." He paused as he got up and walked toward the bed sitting down next to Tawny.

"The guise has been lifted, and I am free to live as I will." He searched her eyes while he spoke seeing the hope and longing flare in them. Taking a deep breath, he opened his own heart and let it show in his eyes.

"If you'll have me, I'm yours. I'll give you the children we've both longed for, if I haven't already. This mutual craving we have for each other will never again go unsatisfied."

"Hell," he made a sound of exasperation, "I'll fuck you day and night if you let me, until we both get a visit from my successor, and no longer have bodies."

He stared down at her expression of anticipation, and finished his plea to be with her for the rest of their lives.

Reaching out to stroke his hand down her sex-tousled hair, he stroked her face as well, making sure her eyes never left his face.

"I love you. The moment I saw you with your grandmother, I knew you were the reason I had taken on the role of Death. Every day, every year, all those decades, that I waited to find the other half of my soul, was worth the torment. I am complete with you, and never want to leave your side. Will you have me?"

He searched her face for any sign she might object, and saw the tears begin to run as she listened to what lived in his heart. His heart suddenly skipped hard, beating a rhythm he hadn't felt since the ancient weapon had been swung at a killing angle. He held his breath, waiting to hear the words that would pronounce sentence on the remainder of his mortal life.

Her simple, teary, "yes" thundered through his heart, washing centuries of loneliness and isolation, leaving a pure love for the woman in front of him in its wake. He knew there wasn't anything he wouldn't brave for the woman who had given him freely the gifts of both life and love.

"Forever." Tawny breathed.

"Forever." Lucas agreed and set about showing her exactly what her gifts meant to him.

Also by Mari Byrne

ઠજ

Death Reborn
Queens' Warriors
Stephanie's Menage

About the Author

෩

Mari currently resides in (mostly) sunny Southern California with her dear husband and two wonderful children. When not writing, she enjoys reading, movies, Japanese anime, vacations (when she can get them), and chocolate. Not always in that order.

Mari welcomes comments from readers. You can find her website and email address on her author bio page at www.ellorascave.com.

Tell Us What You Think

We appreciate hearing reader opinions about our books. You can email us at Comments@EllorasCave.com.

DREAM STALKER
Elisa Adams

ഔ

Chapter 1
ℛ

Alex followed the trail marked by trampled leaves and twigs at her feet. The nearly full moon cast an eerie glow on her surroundings and shadows loomed close in the night around her. The clouds gathering in the night sky promised an evening storm. The faint scent of decay permeated the crisp fall air and marked the presence of the killer. This might be the night that she was finally able to lay all her nightmares to rest.

There was movement just ahead, a stirring in the brush. She was close—closer than she'd ever been. Her pulse raced and her blood pounded through her veins. She took a deep breath and moved forward, silently through the trees. She'd been waiting so long for this moment. All she had to do was reach out and grab it.

For six months it had taunted and teased her. It always remained by her side but just out of her grasp, a constant reminder of what she'd created. This time it was going to be different. *This time* it was her turn. She wasn't going to let it escape again.

Snapping twigs on the path behind her grabbed her attention and distracted her from her goal. *Footsteps.* Her hands clenched into fists and she crouched lower to the ground. Holding completely still, she waited for the intruder to get closer before she attacked.

A quick glance over her shoulder told her it was a man— a human. He was big, but nothing she couldn't handle. She lunged and rammed her shoulder into his legs, knocking him to the ground with a thud. He grunted as his back slammed against the dirt path. In an instant she was on top of him, pinning him to the cold, rocky ground. Her fist connected with his chin, and she felt a sliver of satisfaction when he growled in pain.

"Who are you, and what do you want?" She raised a large rock above her head, poised to bash it into his skull if he didn't give her a reasonable explanation.

"Why, Alexandra Duvall, you never cease to amaze me." The man's voice registered immediately, and her breath stuck in her throat. *Jason Connor.*

She swore under her breath and tried to think of a way to get rid of him. Knowing his personal stake in catching the monster, she should have expected him. She *should* have recognized him sooner.

"Damn it, Jason. Are you trying to get yourself killed?"

"I'm impressed. I didn't think you had it in you. I guess I was wrong. Why don't you put the rock down, sweetheart, and we can catch up on old times. What's it been, four months?"

The amusement she detected in his voice made her want to slam the rock into the side of his head. Instead she let it drop to the ground as she stood up, wanting to put as much distance between them as possible.

"It's been six months, not four, but you already knew that. And let's get one thing straight right now, Jason. If you call me sweetheart one more time, you're going to lose a limb." She kicked a branch out of her way as she started back down the path to where she'd left her car. Thanks to Dr. Know-It-All, she'd lost the trail. The thing was probably long gone by now, and it might be a few days before she caught the trail again.

Damn it. She wanted to ring his big neck. Who did he think he was strutting in here and pretending to know what he was doing? He might be one of the more highly trained researchers in his field, but *she'd* created this monster. If anyone could stop it, it was going to be her.

"Cut the arrogant act, Jason, and go away."

"Leaving so soon?" Jason practically sprang off the ground and stepped in front of her. If he thought his size would intimidate her into cooperating with him, the man had another thing coming.

He leaned his hip against a tree trunk and crossed his arms over his chest. "Where are you rushing off to?"

"I'm going back to my cabin to get some sleep." She sidestepped around him easily. "Thanks to you, I lost my chance at catching that thing tonight."

"I would have had the thing myself if you hadn't been out here snooping around, so don't give me that attitude, Alex." Jason grabbed her arm and pulled her to a stop. "Back off or you're going to get hurt."

She raised her eyebrows at him. "Is that a threat?"

He ran a finger along the underside of her jaw, his expression hot and menacing. His fingers tightened around her arm to the point of near-pain. She took a deep breath to steel her body against the wave of heat that passed through her at his touch. It didn't help. Whenever Jason put his hands on her, her body responded immediately. Instead of shoving him away like she should, she wanted more. She *wanted* his hands on her.

He wound his fingers through her ponytail and pulled her head back, his mouth barely inches from hers. His breath fanned across her lips when he spoke, sending chills down her spine. "It's not a threat, my dear Miss Duvall. It's a promise."

He crushed his mouth down on hers, forcing his tongue into her mouth. There was nothing gentle about the kiss, just as she knew there was nothing gentle about the man. She still ached for him, even now. She brought her arm up around his neck, her fingers tangling in his hair as she pulled him closer. It had been so long, and she'd missed him so much. Her body cried out for more when he broke the kiss.

He held her close for a moment before he pushed her away. It only took a moment for her to come to her senses.

What was she thinking, letting him touch her like that? Why did *she* touch *him?* The answer was clear—she had no choice. When Jason was near, she had no control over her body.

A rustling in the underbrush just ahead of them saved Alex from having to reply. She took off into the trees, streaking through the woods at a breakneck pace to try and catch up with whatever it was in front of her. She broke free of the woods a few minutes later, coming to a stop on the dirt road where she'd left her truck. The killer was nowhere in sight.

"I'm beginning to think you're bad luck, Alex." Jason ran out of the woods and came to a stop next to her. "This is the second time tonight I've missed that thing because of you."

Alex spun on her heel, her hands fisted tightly at her sides. Despite the fact that he had at least eight inches on her and probably outweighed her by a hundred pounds, she knew he'd never really do anything to hurt her—at least not physically. Besides, she'd held her own against much worse than a disgruntled scientist in her lifetime.

"Why don't you just stay out of my way, *Dr. Connor*, and let me do what I came here for. That monster is ruining my life, and it needs to be stopped." She glared at him. "I'm not giving up until that happens."

"Then I guess you're stuck with me, because I'm not about to give up, either." Jason's tone was as arrogant as usual. "You used to work for the Center. You know as well as I do that I have to get this thing. What happened to you was a mistake. When are you going to accept that?"

A mistake? That was the understatement of the year. Jason, Noah Leeds, and the staff at the Leeds Center had made a very big mistake when they released Alex's dream killer from her mind. Now she was paying the consequences.

"You promised to destroy that thing and get it out of my head. I'm going out of my mind." She ran a hand through her hair. "Since you and your cronies from the Leeds Center haven't been able to stop it, I'm going to do it myself."

"That's being mighty hopeful for such a little thing like you." He barked out a laugh. "And you seem to be forgetting something. Noah promised to get rid of that thing. I was just running the machines. And should I mention the fact that you knew the procedure was experimental when you signed up for it? As Noah's research assistant, you went into it with your eyes wide open."

She blew out a breath. Every word he spoke was true, and that's what got her the most. She really didn't have anyone to blame but herself. She'd subjected herself to being the guinea pig for her boss's experiment. No one had forced her into anything. But she wasn't going to stand here and take this crap from a man she used to think cared about her.

"Go to hell, Jason." She started to walk away.

"If I were you, Alex, I'd consider being a little nicer to me." Jason's comment stopped her in her tracks.

"And why would I want to do that?"

"Because I'm your only way out of here tonight, and it's supposed to storm."

She followed his gaze to her truck. When she saw what he was looking at, her heart sank. The windshield was smashed and the tires had been slashed to ribbons. *Damn it.* "Did you do that?"

"I don't need to resort to petty violence. I have much better ways of getting to you, don't I?" He brushed a hand across her neck and she couldn't stop the shiver that coursed through her body. The look in his eyes told her he hadn't missed it, either. "Need a ride, Alex?"

She didn't relish spending any time trapped in a car with him. The man might be a top-notch research scientist, but he had the personality of a doorknob and not enough tact to fill a thimble. He was rude and insulting, and only after one thing from her.

Information.

It didn't help that she'd been head over heels for the guy since day one.

She wanted to tell him she didn't need a ride, or anything else from him. But it was at least a ten mile hike back to her cabin, and it would likely be raining by the time she got there. A low rumble of thunder and a smattering of rain drops made the decision for her. Muttering a low curse, she got into his car.

Chapter 2
ဆ

Jason glanced at Alex out of the corner of his eye. Her dark hair was dusty, littered with crushed leaves and falling out of her ponytail. Her normally fair skin looked deathly pale, but he couldn't get her out of his mind. He'd tried to play it cool with her tonight and take control of the volatile situation, but she just brought out the worst in him. He didn't want to let her get to him, but for her it was almost effortless. It always had been, even before the problems started. She was the only woman he'd ever met who could arouse his passions and his temper in equal measures just as easily.

She stared straight out the windshield, her gaze hard. He smiled, wondering what it would take to get her to look at him. What would she do if he touched her? He *had* to find out. He placed his hand on her thigh. She flinched, but kept her eyes studiously trained on the scenery that passed them by. He caressed her softly. Again she tensed, but her sharp intake of breath coupled with the fact that she didn't move his hand off her leg let him know she didn't want him to stop.

"You know, Alex, it wouldn't kill you to admit that what we had was pretty damned hot." He slid his hand between her legs, just brushing against her mound through her jeans. He was a little surprised that the material felt damp. It bolstered his ego to know she was just as turned on by their wrestling match in the woods as he was.

He brushed against her again, this time a little harder. Her hips jerked and she closed her eyes.

She faced him now, her eyes narrowed and her expression seething. *"Get your hands off me."*

"Is that what you really want?" He cupped her mound in his palm. "I remember how much you used to like my hands on you. In fact, I remember a few times you even begged for them."

She leaned back in the seat, her eyes still squeezed shut. But he didn't miss her flushed cheeks and irregular breathing. She edged her legs apart and he stroked her pussy through her jeans.

Her moan was barely audible, but he didn't miss it. He pulled the car over to the side of the road and shut off the engine.

Alex's gaze snapped to his. "What are you doing?"

"Just giving you what you want. Undo your seatbelt."

Her gaze was wary, but she did as he asked without question. *Smart girl.* He wasn't in the mood to fight with her. He had more important things in mind.

He unzipped her jeans and was surprised that she raised her hips so he could slide them down. She gasped when he pushed his fingers inside her panties. She shook her head, but didn't make any move to stop him. Keeping his gaze locked with hers, he slipped his finger inside her pussy. The expression in her eyes was heated—no longer wary in the least. She whimpered a little and licked her lips when he started to thrust.

The rumble of thunder filled the night air. Alex closed her eyes and swallowed hard. When she opened her eyes he knew the moment had passed. He pulled his hand away from her slowly, brushing his finger across her clit.

"Take me home. *Now.*" Her voice was enraged, but she wasn't unaffected. She straightened out her clothes while he got his car back on the road.

She wanted him. She may not want to, but she did. He would do whatever it took to get her to admit it. He planned to tempt her with another form of stimulation—memories.

"Do you remember that night that we went out to dinner after work? You were so hot by the time we left the restaurant that you couldn't even wait until we got out of the parking lot. You were all over me as soon as we got in the car."

Alex drew in a shuddering breath. "I don't even want to think about that."

Well, *he* did. "You may not want to, but you are." When he glanced at her again she nodded. He reached over to her one more time, his hand brushing across her breast. Through the fabric of her shirt he took the hardened nipple between his thumb and finger and gave it a gentle squeeze before he focused his attention back on the road as his mind traveled back to that night.

Her eyes were on him the entire meal, boring straight into him. He swore she could see right into his soul. He took a sip of his drink, hoping to cool the fires that burned in his throat. As soon as he set the glass down, Alex reached a finger out and caught a drop of liquid that spilled down the side of the glass. She slipped her finger into her mouth and pulled it out slowly, her eyes closed. Jason gripped the edge of the table to keep from grabbing her.

"I'm sorry. I'm being bad." She smiled, not looking sorry at all. "You make me forget how to behave."

God, he wanted to yank the tablecloth and all their dishes off the table and take her right now in full view of everyone. He opened his mouth, but the sudden appearance of her bare toes on his upper thigh rendered him speechless. He hadn't even noticed she'd slipped off her shoes. She scooted down in her seat a little more while her foot slid higher up his thigh. She smiled wickedly when the tips of her toes brushed his cock.

"Alex." His voice was a hoarse whisper as he fought for control of his body and mind. He wanted everything about this night to be perfect. He'd brought her to the most expensive restaurant in the city, tried to impress her in every way imaginable, and yet it was Alex who was showing him a thing or two. When she curled her toes around the length of his straining cock, he signaled for the check. If

he didn't get her home and into bed soon, he was going to have a major problem.

By the time they got out of the restaurant, he wanted to tear her clothes off. It really wasn't anything specific that she did – he'd been feeling this way since well before she decided to show him what she was in the mood for. It was just her. There was something about her that made him feel like his control was an elastic band being stretched to the breaking point. When she touched his cheek as he opened the car door for her, the band snapped.

He sucked in a sharp breath as he closed the door and walked around to the driver's side of the car. If he didn't get control of himself soon, he was going to do something stupid in a public parking lot.

He hadn't even had a chance to buckle his seat belt when her hand was on his thigh. He clenched his hands into fists and tried to pretend she wasn't driving him crazy. He refused to look at her – it would only make the situation worse. "Alex, I think maybe you should keep your hands to yourself until we get back to your place."

"I don't know if I can wait that long."

"We don't have a whole lot of choice. This is a public place." He took a deep breath and glanced her way. Her fair skin was flushed and her lips were parted. She darted her tongue out to wet her bottom lip in a sensual move that set his body on fire. The faint honk of a car horn was nearly drowned out by the blood pounding in his ears, but

it served as a reminder that his behavior was inappropriate.

He mustered all his willpower before he spoke. "We can have the whole night together, but first we have to get out of the parking lot."

She nodded. "Okay. I think you should take me home. Right now."

The urgency in her voice sent him over the edge. Waiting was no longer an option. He beckoned her with his finger. "Come here."

She shot him a nervous glance. "I thought you said you wanted to take me home."

He reached across the console and unbuckled her seat belt, his arm brushing against her breast. He held her gaze as he ran his hand up her thigh, under the hem of her skirt. He skimmed her mound through her panties and was surprised at how wet she was.

"You know I can't stop now." It wasn't a question. She knew as well as he did that it was too late for that. "Besides, I don't think you really want me to. Lift your hips."

She did, and he slid her panties down and off. "Good girl."

The scent of her musk filled the air and it was driving him crazy. His tongue itched to taste her. He wanted to make her come with just his mouth, but that would have to wait for a more private setting. Their activities at this moment would have to be limited to something a little less obvious.

Instead he pushed her legs apart and found her clit with his fingers. He massaged her slowly and she dropped her head back against the headrest. When he slid a finger inside her pussy she moaned. "Jason."

"I want to touch you everywhere." He leaned in and kissed her jaw. She turned to face him and their lips met in a powerful kiss. She sighed against his lips and dug her fingers into his leg, her teeth sinking into his lower lip and her hips grinding against his hand. He didn't know how much more of this he could take before he came in his slacks.

With a deep breath he pulled his hand away from her and reclined his seat back to get comfortable. He unzipped his pants to give some relief to his straining cock. In seconds her hand was on him, freeing his cock from his briefs and stroking him with the tips of her fingers. He grabbed her wrist to stop her. If she kept touching him there was no way he was going to last until he was inside her. And he planned on being inside her very soon.

He pulled her into his lap, hiking her skirt past her hips and praying there was no one nearby to witness what they were about to do. Their boss would definitely look down on them getting arrested.

She ran her hand up and down his cock a few times before she positioned him at the entrance of her pussy and sank down on top of him. He groaned at the sheer rightness of the act. He lifted her up and brought her back down again with excruciating slowness, wanting to savor the feeling of being sheathed inside her hot, wet body.

Alex leaned over and traced the line of his jaw with her tongue, sending shivers through his body. He thrust into her harder, no longer caring if there was anyone watching. This was a once-in-a-lifetime opportunity, and he'd hate himself forever if he passed up something so good.

Jason reached his hand between them and found her clit with his thumb. She whimpered and sank her teeth into his neck. The pain only added more pleasure to their erotic fun. He thrust into her as hard as he could, trying to fill her completely with his cock. A car door slammed near them, maybe in the next parking space, and he knew they had to finish this soon. He held her clit between his thumb and forefinger and squeezed, thrusting hard into her pussy at the same time.

She came almost immediately, her body convulsing over him and her inner muscles clenching around his cock. He thrust into her again and again until he finally lost control. He came hard, his entire body shaking. It was like being struck by lightning. He felt numb all the way to his toes.

He pulled her to him and kissed her hard and fast. "That was incredible."

She nodded her voice breathless. "Yeah." Her hair was in tangles, her bangs plastered to her forehead from the sweat that coated her brow. Her eyelids were heavy and her lips dark pink from their kisses. Her skirt was bunched around her waist and the top two buttons of her shirt had come undone sometime during their brief encounter. He'd never seen anything more beautiful in his life.

He rolled down the fogged-up window to get some air, thankful that he hadn't parked under a street light. Alex ran her fingers through his hair and kissed his chin before she slid back into her own seat to adjust her clothes. It was then that he realized he would do anything to keep her. She was the first woman to excite him so much that he lost all control, and he couldn't let her slip through his fingers.

But he had. He'd lost his objectivity, and he'd gotten careless. Noah had told him over and over again that he wasn't responsible for letting the killer loose, that it was an equipment malfunction. But Jason couldn't let go of the idea that if he'd been paying more attention to the sensors on the machine instead of fantasizing about what he was going to do to her when he got her back to his place, the killer wouldn't have slipped through the portal between her dream and reality. If he'd noticed what had happened just a few seconds earlier, he may have been able to stop it.

She'd told him she didn't blame him, but he knew better. She grew cold and spiteful, and he knew he deserved every second of it. It wasn't long after that night Alex walked out of his life for good.

He *had* to get her back.

When they got to her cabin, Alex jumped out of the car before he even had a chance to put it in park.

"Thanks for the ride."

"Wait, Alex—"

She slammed the door and ran up the steps into the cabin.

Jason got out of the car and followed her inside just as a bolt of lightning streaked across the sky. The lights in the cabin flickered a few times before they went out, the moonlight streaming through the windows the only source of light.

Alex was standing a few feet away, her arms wrapped around her and her body shivering badly. She hated storms, and she hated the dark even more. He wanted to reach out to her, but he didn't dare. Instead he forced his feet to stay firmly planted where he was. "Are you okay?"

She looked at him for a moment before she answered. "Yeah, I'm fine."

She walked over to him and brushed a hand through his hair. Her fingers came away tinged with blood. "You're hurt."

He shrugged. "I hit a tree when you attacked me in the woods. It's nothing serious."

Alex sighed and grabbed a dishtowel off the counter. She pressed it to his head and held it in place with one hand while she picked leaves and twigs from his hair with the other.

"I'm sorry I attacked you. You shouldn't have snuck up on my like that." She shook her head. "Why don't you go sit down on the couch so I can take a look at this?"

He let out a breath and took a step back. "Its fine, Alex."

Her hand dropped to his chin, lingering but just barely touching. Her gentle touch became a caress, sending little shivers of electricity up his spine. When her hands were on him, it was like the past six months had never happened—they hadn't been separated at all. He drew in a sharp breath and wondered if she understood what her touch was doing to him.

"Sorry." She dropped the towel and started to back away, but he snared her wrist and pulled her against him so that her chest was flush with his.

"Don't go anywhere. I want you to keep touching me."

Heat flashed in her gaze, but she hid it quickly. She looked down at the ground for a second, and when her eyes met his again they were filled with hard determination. She was resisting him with everything she had, and it was killing him. What was it going to take to get her to trust him again?

"Please, Alex. I need your hands on me."

"Jason, don't," she pleaded, but she didn't pull away.

He took advantage of her position to brush a kiss across her forehead. "Why not?"

She was silent for longer than he could stand, her eyes trained on the floor. He could feel the awareness humming around her, seeming to take on a life of its own. Yet she refused to acknowledge its existence. "Talk to me, Alex."

"What we had was amazing, but it would be better for both of us if we left it buried in the past where it belongs." Her voice was soft, sad almost, and he didn't believe a word of it. She didn't want to let go any more than he did. There was something else bothering her, and he intended to find out exactly what it was. *Later.* Right now they had some unfinished business to take care of.

"We could have had something great." He brushed his fingertips along her hairline while he placed his other hand on one curvy hip and drew her closer. Heat radiated off her body and whispered across his skin, practically scorching his soul. He *needed* her.

She shook her head. "It never would have worked. I've moved on with my life."

No, she hadn't. And he was going to prove it.

"That's too bad, Alex, because I'm definitely not ready to let this die."

His lips descended upon hers without giving her time to protest. With a quick kiss, a single sweep of his tongue, he set out to claim what was his—what had rightfully belonged to him since that first night in his car.

Alex pulled away, but did nothing to hide the raw desire that flashed in her eyes. He thought he was finally getting through to her, but she sighed and shook her head.

"You should leave now, Jason. I need a shower. In case you haven't noticed I'm covered with mud from rolling around in the woods."

The moment had passed. But he didn't worry too much. There would be plenty more before the night was over.

"We should talk," he said, "about the Center, and about us. I want to know what's going on with you. There's something I need to know."

She tilted her head to the side and pursed her lips. "What now?"

"I want to know about the killer." He held up a hand when she would have stopped him from speaking. "How the hell do you keep finding it when the computers at the Center can't seem to track it for more than a few hours at a time?"

She looked away and took a deep breath, blowing it out noisily. "That's a really long story."

He shrugged. "Hey, I've got all night."

Alex's eyes widened. "You're *not* staying."

"I am, at least until I get some answers."

"Then you're going to have to wait ten minutes." She turned on her heel and walked into the bathroom. "Wait here. We'll talk in a bit." She shut the bathroom door, and a few minutes later Jason heard her turn the shower on.

Patience was not one of his strong suits. He paced the room restlessly for all of five minutes before he decided to join her.

Chapter 3

ജ

Alex stood under the hot spray of the shower, letting the scalding water ease some of the tension in her back. Seeing Jason again, *touching* him again, flooded her mind with memories she'd all but forgotten. She'd tried to forget him, but even six months apart hadn't put a dent in the ache she felt whenever she thought about him.

Now he was here, just a few feet beyond the bathroom door. She knew he wanted to pick up where they left off. Maybe she wanted that, too. She didn't know if it was possible after all that had happened, but being so close to him made her want to try.

She was only mildly surprised when she heard the bathroom door open. She hadn't invited him to join her, but she'd known that Jason never bothered to wait for an invitation. He took what he wanted—and if it was *her* that he wanted, she wasn't going to put up a fight. Much.

A thrill shot through her when she heard the rasp of his zipper over the water. The man had the most amazing cock, and he definitely knew how to use it. She'd never had so many screaming orgasms in her life as she'd had with him.

The metal curtain rings jingled softly as he pulled back the curtain and stepped into the shower. She smiled to herself at the thought of Jason naked, standing inches away from her. She didn't bother to turn around since it would have been nearly impossible to see him with the lights out. But she didn't need to see him for a vivid picture of his body to form in her mind. She was dripping with cream before he even touched her.

She should tell him to go away, but they both knew that wasn't going to happen. As much as she hated to admit it, she had missed him.

She made a token protest, knowing he wouldn't back away. "I told you to wait in the other room."

"I've never really been very good at following directions." He stepped closer, the heat from his body radiating against the skin of her back. Steam from the shower hung in air filled with the scent of soap and her own musk. She drew the washcloth in her hand slowly across her breasts and whimpered as the rough fabric scraped across her sensitized nipples.

He placed his hands on her hips and squeezed gently. "What fun would it be to always follow the rules?"

She nearly moaned when she felt his breath fan across her neck. "None at all."

He kissed her shoulder, his lips sliding over her wet skin. "Can you honestly tell me you don't want this, Alex?"

Lying would be a mistake. "No."

"I didn't think so."

"Awfully sure of yourself, aren't you, Dr. Connor?"

Jason brushed his fingertip over one of her tight nipples. He caught the hard tip between his fingers and pinched. "I think I have a good reason to be."

She shamelessly arched her back to push her breast further into his hand. "I never could resist you."

When he spoke again his voice was a low growl. "I know."

He pushed her wet hair over her shoulder and brought his lips to her neck. The little nips he rained over her skin made her shudder with desire. The combination of the water beating across her front and Jason's enticing warmth so near to her back almost made her come undone.

Jason traced the shell of her ear with his tongue and whispered to her. "It's been six months since I've tasted you. Do you know how hard it's been for me to be without you?"

"No," she lied. She *did* know. It had been hell living without him, every night her body crying out for his touch.

He grabbed her hips and dragged her roughly back against him so that his erect cock pressed into her back. She wriggled against him and he groaned. "It's been *this* hard, Alex. Just thinking about you was torture."

She understood that all too well. He cupped her breasts in his hands and plucked her nipples until they ached. His hands skimmed down the wet flesh of her abdomen until he found her mound. She moved her legs apart wantonly to make room for his searching fingers.

By the time he turned her around to face him, her body had turned into molten liquid ready to pool at his feet. He leaned down and took one of her throbbing nipples between his lips. He tortured her gently with his teeth and tongue until she could barely breathe. Her body was screaming out for the kind of release only Jason could give her, but he seemed content to play with her breasts instead.

"Please, Jason."

He looked up from his fun, his eyes gleaming. "Please, what?"

"I need you now," she rasped, her legs nearly giving out.

"Patience, sweetheart. We have six months to catch up on." He pressed her back against the shower wall and nudged her legs apart, his hand trailing up her inner thigh. When he reached her mound he brought his hand back down and started over again. She grabbed his hand, intent on putting him right where she needed him to be, but Jason had other ideas. He took the washcloth from her hand and coated it with soap.

He slipped it between her legs, following the same path he had moments ago traveled with just his hand. This time he didn't stop. He brushed the cloth lightly against her mound before he started the process again.

Each time he pressed harder, lingered longer, until his hand stayed against her. She rocked her hips against him, trying to end the torment he was inflicting upon her.

"Is this what you want?" He rubbed the cloth against her clit. She almost came right then.

"*Yes!*"

"Good. It's what I want, too." He caressed her clit with the cloth while his lips once again found her nipple. She was so sensitive from his earlier attention that she screamed. Her body racked with convulsions as she came, her legs dropping out from under her. He caught her when she would have fallen, quickly turned off the faucet, and carried her out of the bathroom to the carpeted floor in the next room. He laid her down on the floor and held her until her body stopped trembling from the aftershocks of the incredible climax.

After a little while she came back to her senses and felt his cock pressed against her thigh. She took him in her hand, stroking him slowly. He closed his eyes and groaned.

She kissed his cheek. "Why don't you lay back and make yourself more comfortable?"

Jason nodded and reclined back on the rug, his cock jutting into the air. His breathing was heavy and uneven and his hips jerked every time she brushed against him. A drop of pre-cum glistened on the tip of his cock and she leaned down to lick it off.

"Oh God, Alex." His hips jerked hard, thrusting his cock against her lips. She swirled her tongue around the head a few times before taking him into her mouth. He tasted exactly like she remembered. She watched him closely as she stroked his cock with her lips and tongue. His eyes remained closed, his lips parted and his face pleasantly flushed. He didn't last more than a minute before he pushed her away, stood up, and carried her to the bed.

He laid her down on her stomach and ran a hand over her back. He squeezed her ass and she wriggled, wanting him inside her. She raised her hips and he took the hint, lifting her hips and dragging her up onto her hands and knees.

He moved her legs apart and took her from behind, his cock sliding into her pussy until his balls smacked against her. He thrust into her hard and fast while his fingers played with her clit. One of his hands tangled in her hair while the other remained on her hip to hold her in place for his thrusts.

She hadn't been with anyone else since she'd left him. She hadn't wanted anyone else. The feeling of his thick cock inside her stretching her and filling her completely made her feel whole again.

"Come for me, Alex," he growled. "I can't wait much longer."

She felt his urgency as if it were her own. Another flick of his finger and she came, stars exploding in front of her eyes. That's the way it always was with him. It probably always would be.

Jason came soon after, his body shuddering. Alex's arms sagged as he leaned more of his weight on her. He kissed the center of her back before he withdrew his cock from her sated pussy, lifting her up and standing her on her feet. Her hair, still wet from the shower, dripped water that was now ice cold down her body. She shivered as the rivulets ran down her breasts and her stomach.

Jason gave her a quick kiss. "Wait here. I'll go get some towels."

She kept her eyes on his tight ass as he walked into the bathroom. As he returned with the towels and dried her off, she wondered if he planned to stay the whole night.

Chapter 4

ဆ

Jason rummaged through the cabinets, his cell phone propped between his ear and his shoulder, only half-listening to his boss rant and rave about his inability to do his job.

"Did you get the killer yet?" Noah's tone was harsh and demanding. Jason rolled his eyes.

He pinched the bridge of his nose. "No, not yet." *Coffee. He needed caffeine — couldn't function without it.*

"Well, what are you waiting for?"

"Do you really think that creature is just going to jump right into my arms?" He gave a silent cheer when he finally found a can of coffee shoved in the back corner of the fridge. "Get real, Noah."

"You have three more days. Then I'll have to find someone else to do it." Noah sighed. "Can you get Alexandra to help you?"

Jason set up the coffee maker and turned it on, giving silent and heartfelt thanks that the electricity had come back on sometime during the night. "I'm working on it."

"Whatever. Look Jason, I don't have time for games. If that monster isn't caught, the wrong people are going to find out about the dream research we've been doing. If that happens, the Center will probably be shut down. Tom and I have put too much work into this project to watch it go down the tubes now. Just find the killer before someone else does."

Noah hung up before Jason could reply.

"Who was that?"

He turned to find Alex right behind him. He considered lying to her, but he didn't think she'd buy it. "Noah."

She nodded. "That's what I thought. Is everything okay?"

"Yeah, fine," he lied. Nothing was okay. He was on the verge of losing his job and probably his sanity, but that didn't matter to him as much as the fact that Alex was standing in front of him wearing nothing more than a bed sheet. Suddenly even caffeine didn't seem so important.

She brushed his hair off his forehead. "Your cut looks much better."

"Like I said, it's just a scratch." He actually had a mild headache, but he wasn't going to admit that to her.

She reached past him to get a mug from the cabinet. "What did Noah want?" Her voice was casual as she filled the mug with coffee, but tension radiated off of her in droves.

"You already know that answer." He took a deep breath. This wasn't going to be easy. "I think we should talk about the connection you apparently still have with the killer."

Alex looked away. "How did you know about that?"

"It's pretty obvious. You always seem to know where it is."

She nodded and snorted a laugh. "I've got to tell you, this treatment of Noah's is a crock."

"Why is that?" He knew there had been some problems in Noah's and his partner, Tom Crandall's, research, but they hadn't wanted to listen to him about any of it. Still, Jason should have put his foot down and not let Alex get involved.

"He's promising to help free people from their nightmares, touting this treatment as better than any anxiety medication." She paused and looked out the window. "It's a great theory, but there's one major flaw. The killer still haunts my dreams at night. Except now he taunts me, tells me he's free but I'll never be. Before he was just a figment of my imagination. Now he's alive, and he can do whatever he wants. So in reality, I've created this terrible thing and released it upon the world."

If he'd known that she still had close contact with the killer during her dreams, they could have stopped it. Since the accident in the lab with Alex, Noah and Tom had been working around the clock to perfect the treatment. If she'd just stuck around another month, the whole six month separation could have been avoided. "Why didn't you tell me what was going on?"

Her answer surprised him. "I didn't want you to get hurt."

A tear rolled down her cheek, a rare occurrence for her that stirred his protective instincts. He pulled her tight against his body and kissed the top of her head. "It's going to be fine, Alex."

"I really hope so." She bit her lower lip and set her mug down on the counter. "But I don't really want to think about it right now."

Her breasts, covered only in the thin sheet, pressed against his bare chest. She scraped her fingernail lightly over his flat nipple, eliciting a soft moan from his lips. He figured she must have dreamed about the killer again and was looking for a distraction. He could provide that, for a little while. Then they had to get to work.

He leaned back against the counter and closed his eyes. His mind drifted back to the shower they'd shared, and everything that had happened after. Within seconds he had a hard-on that could break concrete.

"Alex," he whispered as her hands found the zipper of his jeans, the only article of clothing he'd bothered to put on when his phone rang early this morning.

"Is there something you want to say?" She slipped her fingers inside his pants and caressed his cock.

"I have many things I want to tell you." He caught her earlobe with his teeth between words. "Let me start with the fact that you're making me crazy with those fingers."

"That's my intention." She let the sheet drop and he was treated to the sight of nothing but skin, her generous curves bared to him in the daylight.

All thoughts of getting caffeine into his bloodstream fled when Alex caressed her bare nipples. The little moans that escaped her throat drove him crazy. After a moment he caught her hands and brought them to his hips.

"I want you bad, Alex." He kissed her, slowly and thoroughly, while he pressed his groin against hers. She slid his jeans down his hips so that his cock pressed against the flesh of her stomach.

"I can tell." When she laughed, his cock pushed harder against her.

He stepped out of his jeans and kicked them aside, needing them out of the way. He thought briefly about taking her back to bed for the morning, but vetoed the idea quickly. Instead he lifted her by the hips and set her down on the table.

She leaned back on her hands and spread her legs slowly, giving him an enticing and incredibly arousing show. He breathed deeply and fitted himself between her legs to rub the tip of his cock against her clit. Alex moaned and raised her hips. "I want you inside me now, Jason."

He shook his head. Not yet. He moved away from her and leaned over so that his mouth was scant inches from her labial lips. She cried out when his tongue touched her gently. He leaned closer and inhaled her musky scent before he separated her lips with his thumbs and found her clit with his tongue.

He stroked her gently a few times, his gaze stuck on the trickle of juice that escaped her pussy. Unable to resist, he followed the trail with his tongue and then thrust it inside her.

He flicked her clit with his finger while he thrust his tongue inside her until he felt her quiver. She threw her head back and screamed when she came. Still, he didn't lift his mouth from her. She gripped him by the hair and pulled him away.

He stood up and kissed her, thrusting his tongue into her mouth. He wrapped his arms around her and crushed her against him.

She reached between them and grasped his cock in her hand. Her thumb swirled over the tip, spreading around the pre-cum that had gathered there, while her other hand grabbed his ass. When she dug her fingernails into his skin he groaned.

Alex bit his earlobe. "You make me feel so good, Jason."

He barked out a laugh as she increased the pressure on his cock. "It's definitely mutual."

He brushed her hand out of the way and slid his cock into her pussy. Her hips rocked against him and she moaned. He tangled his hands in her hair and held on tight. Alex wrapped her legs around his waist, her heels digging into his ass to pull him closer still. He looked down between them to watch his cock slide in and out of her. The sight turned him on even more.

God, he'd missed her. This time he wasn't going to stand by and watch her leave. If she decided to go, he was going to follow her until she came to her senses. They belonged together, whether or not she chose to accept it.

He leaned in and whispered into her ear. "I love you, Alex."

She smiled. "I love you, too."

He was momentarily stunned by her unhesitant reply. He stopped moving and stared at her. "Yeah?"

"Yeah." When she laughed her inner muscles clenched him tightly, spurring him into thrusting again. This time it was with much more force—he could feel his orgasm fast approaching.

She loved him. He'd never known that. It had to be one of the most erotic things Alex had ever said to him. He hoped he'd have the chance to hear it again, many times.

He thrust into her one last time before he fell apart, his mind and soul shattering with an intense orgasm. He leaned in and kissed her as she came, her body shuddering against and around his. She collapsed into him, her breathing labored. Her hands stroked his shoulders, slowly and gently.

His mind raced and his blood still burned through his veins. When he'd gone in search of her, this wasn't what he'd expected to happen. He hadn't even let himself give in to the hope that they could be together again. Now that he had Alex in his arms, where she belonged, he'd have to figure out a way to keep her there.

* * * * *

"Do you want to tell me about the nightmares?"

Jason's question took her by surprise. "Hasn't Noah told you everything you need to know?"

"He's given me the basic information." Jason looked up from his laptop, his demeanor entirely business. It was almost as if they hadn't made wild passionate love just an hour ago. "But definitely not everything I need to know."

When the man worked, he *worked*. He shut down to everything around him and concentrated on the task at hand. She hid a smile, remembering how different he'd been at work and away from it. She wondered if anyone else at work had any idea of how passionate he could be about something other than his job.

Alex blew out a breath. "The dreams started not long after my parents were killed. I was so young, so afraid, and I made their killer into this monster in my mind. When Noah offered me a way to free myself of the nightmares, I jumped at the chance. I didn't know he planned on releasing my nightmare monster into the world."

"That was a mistake." Jason went back to his work, his fingers tapping the keys as he worked on the program he told her would trap the killer as Noah had originally intended. "He really did want to help; he just didn't expect your nightmares to be so vivid. Noah's not a bad guy; he's just a little obsessed with work."

Just like someone else she knew. "What he meant to do isn't important right now. Until the killer is destroyed, I won't be able to live in peace. And I can't let you take it back to the Center for Tom to study it. I don't want to chance it getting loose again."

He shook his head. "Noah's not getting it. No one is. This thing has no place in a research facility. It's too dangerous. But if I don't stop it a lot of people are going to die."

"I'm going to help you." She'd waited too long for this to be shoved aside.

"I can't let you do that. I care too much about you to knowingly put you in harm's way."

She sighed. If he thought she was going to give up without a fight, he underestimated her. "You don't have a choice. Either we work together, or I do this alone."

"Don't do this."

She heard the warning in his tone. "I do what I have to do. In fact, I don't even need you at all."

Jason sighed and looked at her, his eyebrows raised. "Would you care to tell me how you plan to stop this monster by yourself?"

Alex smiled. "Gladly."

Chapter 5

ജ

She walked across the room slowly to the dresser, reached into a drawer and pulled out a small, intricate box. It was a ruby-red glass with sparkling gems covering most of the surface. Jason narrowed his eyes and studied the thing, wondering how she planned to stop a seemingly invincible killer with a box that was no bigger than an apple. When he looked at her, he saw she was smiling.

"What the hell is that?"

"When I was three and I first started having terrible nightmares, my mother found a box just like this at a magic shop. She told me it was a dream box, and I could use it to trap my nightmares so they wouldn't bother me again."

"Did it work?"

She nodded. "Until she was murdered. Then the nightmares got out of control."

"So what makes you think it's going to work now?"

"Because I've begun to realize that, even though the killer is loose, it's still a product of *my* imagination. *I* can control *it*."

"And you think a *magic box* is going to stop a monster that the most sophisticated scientific equipment couldn't catch?"

She nodded. "I know it will."

Yeah, right. He wondered if she'd gone over the deep end. "Give me another ten or fifteen minutes and I'll have this program ready to go. It's basically the same one we use at the Center, but on a smaller scale. All the bugs have been worked out since the last time you were subjected to it."

"Okay. I'll wait over here."

Jason glanced up at her, wondering where the sudden complacency had come from. Was she planning something without him? He didn't want her risking her neck when he had all the answers to her problems literally at the tips of his fingers…

With any luck, Alex wouldn't need to wait for Jason's program. She could feel the sleeping pills she had taken a little while ago beginning to work. She clutched the dream box tighter in her hand as she lay down on the bed. She wasn't going to put Jason in danger if she didn't have to. She'd seen one of these boxes work before, felt the power of trapping a dream stalker with her own hands, and she *was* going to make it work again.

She thought about Jason as she drifted off to sleep, hoping she'd be back to see him again.

* * * * *

"Alexandra."

Alex opened her eyes when she heard her name whispered. The sleeping pills had worked quickly. She was standing in the living room of her childhood home. No lights were on and the room was bathed only in moonlight.

"Alexandra."

She spun around to see a dark shadow in the corner of the room. She squeezed her hands into fists, the corners of the dream box biting into her palm.

"Help me." The killer had a voice that sounded like nails on a chalkboard. It grated in her ears and made her want to scream. But she had to keep control of herself or she would end up dead.

"What do you want from me?"

The killer stepped out of the shadows. Alex sucked in a breath at the sight of it. Even after all these years it still shocked her. Well over seven feet tall, the creature created in her imagination had straggly black hair that partially covered a misshapen face. Its skin was an angry red and in the place of its eyes were empty black sockets.

"I want you dead." The killer took another step closer. It raised a huge, bony hand in her direction and she flinched.

She held the dream box out of sight, needing to stall for time until it got closer.

It walked slowly forward until it came to a stop just in front of her. The stench of decay that permeated from every pore in its body filled the air and made her want to vomit.

"I've wanted you dead for years." Its eye sockets glowed white when it spoke. "Now I'm free to do it."

Just as it reached out for her she opened her palm, revealing the box. The creature hissed. "*That* can't hold me anymore."

"It may not have held you for long when I was a kid, but things are different now." She pressed a button on the front of the box and the lid popped open. "I'm not a kid now. I don't believe in you anymore."

A swirl of air escaped the box and surrounded the creature. Its scream was unearthly as it was turned into vapor and sucked inside the box. Alex flipped the lid shut, shuddering with the power of releasing herself from her worst nightmare. The dream box shook in her hands a few times before it stilled.

"Good job."

She turned and found Jason standing in the doorway.

"How did you get here?"

"I told you to give me a few minutes with the computer program." He walked over to her and pulled her into his arms. He smelled like life, like *reality*, and it was incredible. She couldn't wait to wake up. "You shouldn't have risked yourself like that."

She held up the box. The gems embedded in the colored glass now glowed almost neon in the dark room. "I had to do it myself. It was the only way. That was the major flaw in Noah's plan. Only the person having the nightmares can release them from their mind."

Jason was silent for a minute while he thought about what she said. He finally laughed and shook her lightly. "You still should have waited for me, but I understand the need to do it on your own. I'm glad you're safe."

She shrugged. "I told you I could do it."

She raised her arm and threw the dream box at the far wall. When it hit, it shattered into hundreds of pieces. She was finally free.

Chapter 6

ಬ

"When you're finished with that research, I need you to take this file to the fourth floor for Tom to have a look at."

Alex looked up when a file was dropped on her desk and stared at her boss. She picked up the file and shoved it back into his hands. "Get a life, Noah. I have a lunch date."

Noah shook his head. "Then I guess I'll have to do it myself. Just don't be late again like you were last week."

Jason walked into her office and leaned a hip against her desk. "I'll bring her back on time if you promise to let her out a little early tonight."

Noah crossed his arms over his chest and raised a dark eyebrow. "You know as well as I do that the dream box research has to be done by next week or the patient appointments will have to be postponed. Neither Tom nor I want to see that happen, not when we've worked for the past six months to incorporate those silly boxes into the program. We're still trying to find a manufacturer that can produce more than ten or twenty a month."

She wasn't about to mention to Noah that her "silly box" did something none of his fancy equipment had been able to do.

Jason winked at her before turning back to Noah. "Letting Alex have a night off isn't going to cause a setback."

"It just might." Noah shook his head. "As a matter of fact, I think you should both stay for a few extra hours tonight. The deadline for the project is approaching and we could use all the help we can get."

Alex sighed. She'd agreed two months ago to come back to the Leeds Center because she thought the insights she'd gained from her experiences might help others. Now she wondered of it would have been better to find another job. Noah's workaholic behavior was going to drive her to the brink of madness before the dream project even got off the ground. To think she used to wonder why he wasn't married.

"Sorry, Noah. Not tonight." When Jason turned to face Alex, his smile was wicked. "I have plans for you."

She returned his smile with one of her own. "I can't wait."

* * * * *

Alex woke up the next morning wrapped in Jason's arms. She let herself wake up slowly, enjoying the feeling of being relatively well-rested now that the nightmares had stopped.

She looked over at Jason and saw that he was watching her through half-closed eyes.

"Good morning, sleepyhead."

He laughed. "It's your fault for waking me up in the middle of the night." He kissed the side of her neck and nuzzled her hair.

She started to climb out of bed, but his heavy arm over her abdomen stopped her. "It's already seven o'clock, Jason. I don't want to be late for work."

His smile was rakish. "I thought maybe we could call in sick and spend the day in bed."

"As appealing as that sounds, we have responsibilities." She finally managed to move his arm off her.

"I'll let you off the hook on one condition."

She raised her eyebrows at him. "And what would that be?"

"Marry me."

He propped his upper body on his elbows to look at her when she didn't answer. "It doesn't have to be any big deal. We can go to city hall if you want."

She sat up and shook her head. "Are you serious?"

"Yes, but I don't want to force you into anything you don't want to—"

"Okay."

He stared at her, his expression wary. "Okay?"

"Yes." She kissed his nose.

He blinked a few times before a slow smile spread across his face. "Now I'm going to have to call Noah and tell him we'll be a little late. We have some celebrating to do."

He pulled her back down on the bed and kissed her deeply.

Also by Elisa Adams

❧

Claiming Kate
Complicated
Hold
Inescapable
Renaissance

About the Author

ഇ

Born in Gloucester, Massachusetts, Elisa Adams has lived most of her life on the east coast. Formerly a nursing assistant and phlebotomist, writing has been a longtime hobby. Now a full time writer, she lives on the New Hampshire border with her husband and three children.

Elisa welcomes comments from readers. You can find her website and email address on her author bio page at www.ellorascave.com.

Tell Us What You Think

We appreciate hearing reader opinions about our books. You can email us at Comments@EllorasCave.com.

SCORCHED DESTINY
Michelle Pillow

ഔ

Chapter One
Modern Day
And one shall free him by succumbing to the passions
within…

🔊

"You're in the wrong desert. You do know that, don't you, Miss Luci? If you're looking for one of the djinn, you should be looking in the Arabian desert not the Sahara." Mr. Randolph Turner swabbed his head before shoving his ridiculous hat back on top of it. Who wore a British flag sun visor in the desert anyway? "Now, it's clear to me you don't know what you're doing. Your father wants you to come home. It's a generous offer and I think you should take it. Let's both get out of this Godforsaken land."

Lucienne de la Rue stopped walking and took a deep breath. Her boots sank down into the uneven sand of the desert. The grainy landscape went on for miles, like a golden, ever-changing ocean. Sweat plastered her white linen shirt to her body and she'd pretty much given up on the idea of staying clean. Water was scarce as it was, and she'd rather drink it than bathe in it. Her mother and sister would be appalled. Her father would call it an obsession. Lucienne thought of it as a small sacrifice on the way to meeting her destiny.

She'd gotten her stubborn hardheadedness from her father. They never got along because of it. Henry de la Rue wanted her to run his company, which specialized in ancient artifacts and antiquities. He'd turned the family obsession and generations of research into a profitable business.

Lilliana, her mother and Violette, her younger sister, were as debutante as they got. They were the last of a dying breed of socialites. Lucienne was anything but.

According to her prim and proper mother, Lucienne dressed like a man—in slacks, a pale linen shirt, boots and a vest. She grinned, knowing she could act like a man too when times called for it. The wind blew a long wisp of her turban free, taking a long strand of her dark hair with it, and she automatically pushed the black material over her shoulder. She found the headdress much more suited to the environment than a hat, and at times it helped her to hide the fact that she was indeed female.

Hitting her dusty gloves along her thigh, Lucienne turned to look at Mr. Turner. He was a short, balding man with bad teeth and a questionably low IQ. She'd put up with him when he insisted that rewarding men with champagne was a good idea—men who incidentally dug outside in the desert sun all day afterward. Because of him she'd lost a whole team of workers to heatstroke. She put up with him when he insisted on horses instead of camels, when he complained about the accommodation in his tent, when he complained about the hot sun, the blistering winds and the chilly desert nights.

Lucienne put up with him because he was the man her father sent to check on her. Henry had started sending her funds now that her own had run out. Mr. Turner was the man who reported to her father whether or not she was close to finding what she was looking for. But now Mr. Turner was going to question her? All because he apparently cracked open a book and read a few passages about "genies". Maybe he should've tried an atlas first.

"With the pretty looks that run in your family, there's no reason you couldn't find a nice man like your sister has and settle down," Mr. Turner continued. Lucienne tried not to gag at the thought. The man's tone lowered an octave, "You have your mother's blue eyes and dark brown hair and your father's proud features."

Mr. Turner was looking at her and smiling. Was he trying to come on to her?

No, he's trying to come on to my father's fortune.

For two months she'd tolerated this man dogging her every move, only to come to one conclusion. Out of all the men her father sent, this one was the worst. Mr. Turner was a complete, incompetent idiot. And she was tired of him.

Her voice hard, she stared the little man down. "The east Sahara is split up into three regions. The Libyan Desert extends from the Nile valley to west Egypt and east Libya. The Nubian Desert is in northeast Sudan. And the Arabian Desert, Mr. Turner, rests between the Red Sea and the Nile valley. Take a good look around. You're standing in the Arabian, Mr. Turner. You have been for two months. I suggest you ask where you're going next time my father puts you on his private jet and hands you a wad of cash."

A few of the diggers she'd hired laughed as her words were translated for them. She understood their words because her grandmother had taught her many of the desert languages—at least enough to get by. Mr. Turner said nothing but stood and glared at her.

"Now," Lucienne continued, "over that dune is another dune and beyond that another. Feel free to walk back to the States and tell my father to shove his offer up his ass. By the time you get there, I'll have my artifact. Now, if you don't feel like taking a stroll, sit your narrow butt down and shut the hell up!"

Don't give up. Destiny awaits you. You were meant to wake him, a small voice in her head said. She'd heard the voice before and assumed it to be her conscience.

Lucienne took a deep breath. She was close. She could feel it. All those years sitting at her grandmother's knee, listening to the story of how their family was destined to free the djinn race and receive great riches and happiness.

She'd thought they were only stories until she found her grandfather's journal—a leatherbound volume full of research and historical facts, of her ancestors plight through the ancient desert sands. The tale was as hard and stirring as the desert itself. Her grandfather had died looking for the "lost ones" as did his father and the many fathers before them. For generations, the men in her family had searched until her father. Henry didn't believe in the djinn or the foretold strength of their powers. He believed his daughter was wasting her time and her life.

Lucienne not only wanted the riches promised, but her heart bled for the poor, trapped souls. She had no idea how many djinn there were, but somehow she'd help them. The need burned within her, pushing aside everything else—every desire, every need or want. She dreamed about it at night, thought of nothing else during the day. Perhaps her father was right. Perhaps she had gone mad like those before her.

Or maybe that smelly Englishman in Cairo had it figured out. Maybe all she needed was a man to give her a good, hard "shagging" to keep her out of trouble. That Englishman wasn't close to what she wanted to have thrusting between her thighs.

She'd be a liar if she didn't admit to herself that the djinn's sexual prowess intrigued her. It was said that just one look at them and a woman could orgasm. Somehow when faced with such a fantasy, mortal men paled in comparison. She'd thought about it a lot and knew that when she found her djinni, she'd be fucking him before she freed him.

At least once in her life, she would know the foretold pleasure of a djinni's embrace. Just thinking about it made her pussy wet and her body heat beyond the gust of desert winds. At any time during the day images would come to her, taunting her, driving her on when she knew she should rest. They were images of dark strong hands on her flesh and bold dark eyes calling to her, burning with an inner fire.

Was it wrong that her mission to save the djinn carried such a selfish, base purpose? Regardless, the fantasy of it drove her out of the beds of other men. The idea of it made her so frustrated with longing that she couldn't see straight and masturbation no longer held any appeal. But there was more to it than passion and sex. Her heart beat for the unknown djinni she would find.

Girlish longing? Fanciful thinking? Insanity? Maybe it was all three.

But, it didn't make Lucienne's feelings any less real. Perhaps that was the true reason she braved the angry desert. She was enamored with a djinni. He came to her in dreams, never really talking as he teased and tormented her body to the point of explosion. She'd wake up with the promise of more, but completely unfulfilled. Masturbating had lost its appeal, though she did that often.

Maybe she was a fool. But then again, who knew? Maybe it was even true love. Maybe the man who haunted her was real, one of the ancient djinn calling to her. She liked to think so.

Lucienne believed in the djinn. She believed with all her heart. That was why she was the first de la Rue female after generations to look for a djinni. And she just knew that she'd be the de la Rue to find one.

Chapter Two
Two Weeks Later

৪১

Lucienne trembled, her legs wobbling as she half stepped, half skidded down the long incline. The stairs to the buried chamber were intact, but they were covered with centuries of desert sand which made walking hard. Ancient hieroglyphics were carved into the walls, barely recognizable. Running her hands over them, she brushed them free of sand to better see them. She remembered enough from her reading to decipher a few words—underworld, gods, cursed. It was probably a warning to turn back.

Lucienne kept going.

As she reached the bottom, the beam of light shot out from her flashlight, breaking up the isolated blackness of the tomblike chamber. The air was still, the room so quiet she could hear her own heart pounding. She was alone, having sent the diggers away to their tents. Lucienne didn't need them anymore. She'd found what she was looking for.

This was it. He was here. Now all she had to do was find him.

Moving her arm, she gasped as the room lit up for a brief second. The flashlight beam had hit metal, reflecting off the shiny surface to give light. Readjusting the beam, she set it in the sand and pointed it at a mirror. A soft glow surrounded her. The chamber was a little less scary with the light. She took the backup flashlight from her pack.

Lucienne stood. The large chamber was a giant rectangle. Large urns lined one wall, undisturbed for centuries. Two rectangles were carved into the ground. She guessed they'd once been pools of water surrounding the walkway she was on.

In the center of the hieroglyphic wall, an oval symbol with three star patterns and a straight line was carved. Her heartbeat quickened. She'd found it. Grandfather had been right. The djinn were buried in tombs—tombs for those caught between the living and the dead—not mortal, but no longer favored by the gods. They were the lost ones, the fallen angels, trapped for all time. If she found one, she'd be able to set into motion the wish that would free them all.

"I knew it," she whispered, stumbling forward only to fall to her knees as she stared at the ancient symbol. She'd waited her whole life for this moment. Every crazy decision she'd made, every last penny she'd spent was now validated by this moment. "I knew it was true."

* * * * *

An hour passed alone in the chamber as Lucienne searched for the secret door that would take her to the hidden room where the djinni was kept. As if drawn by a sudden surge of longing to a wall, she pushed a tiny hieroglyph.

Lucienne jumped back, startled as a secret door unlatched. She waited, breathless, her heart pounding in excitement and fear. This was it. The djinni was close—so close. Taking a deep breath, she braced her arm against the large stone and forced the door open, struggling to find footing on the sandy floor. When it was wide enough to squeeze through, she stopped.

With a grunt she passed through the narrow entry, holding her flashlight in her hand. Unlike the other chamber, the triangular hall was clean and undisturbed. Lucienne felt a tickle on her arm. Thinking it to be a bug, she jerked and brushed her skin, only to stop. It was a strand of her dark brown hair that touched her flesh. Not only that, but her hands were clean of sweat and sand.

"What the…?" Gasping, Lucienne looked down. Her clothes were gone, replaced by a pleated linen dress, very ancient Egyptian in style. A cool metal necklace hugged her neck and a thick bracelet clasped her arm. Her boots were replaced with sandals.

"This is it. He's here. I've found it." The words were so shaky she barely recognized her own voice. "I've found him."

A light breeze hit her. Lucienne had always assumed she was passionate but that her deepest passions were buried deep inside, sleeping. Whatever had touched her in the breeze awoke them all at once, making her excited. The thin, nearly transparent material caressed her skin and she watched her dark nipples bud against the cloth. Suddenly, her pussy was wet, drenched to the heightened state of desperate arousal. Her thighs became damp with her need, her panties gone. Almost frantically, she continued forward, barely noting that the way was lit by torches and that her flashlight had vanished.

It had been so long since she'd had sex and all the energy and frustration she'd felt over the years of searching seemed to surge forth at once. She started running, instinctively knowing that what she sought, what she needed, what was at the end of the hall.

You were meant to wake him, a voice whispered in her head. This time it was more distinct and she understood that it wasn't her conscience but the whisper of fate. *Your life has been lived for this moment. Your female body is the key. That is why the others before you failed.*

Lucienne knew what she had to do. The others before her had been men. According to her grandfather's journal, a man had cursed all the djinn because one of them refused to enslave all women, including the djinni's lover. A man's jealousy and hate had started the djinn imprisonment. It stood to reason that a woman's passion and love would free them of it.

Each movement sent a jolt through her. The breeze hit again, this time stronger. Her body was being prepared. It was like a thousand fingers touched her. Her pussy throbbed, it was so needy and hot. As she stepped into the chamber at the end of the hall, it was like entering a dream—a place where all her fantasies, all her desires could come true. It was a strange understanding that passed over her, an acceptance.

Destiny.

Fate.

For a moment she panicked, scared that the chamber would be empty. And then she saw him, the man of both her destiny and fate. All fear and worry left her. It was the man she'd searched for.

Her djinni.

The man who would be able to sate the burning hunger inside her body.

He looked just as a man of such grace and power should look—beautiful, strong and virile. Orange firelight caressed his naked form, the light flickering over his gorgeous body and tight flesh. Long, blue-black hair fell over his back. He was turned away from her, affording her a lush view of a taut ass and muscled thighs. Not a measure of fat marred his frame and for a moment she thought him too perfect to be real.

Lucienne quickly glanced around his prison. It was made of stone, but covered with red and white gauze. There was a basin of water set high on a pillar. A thick cushioned chair was next to the bed. In the middle of the room was a low, flat bed, covered with fine silks and surrounded by translucent material hanging from the ceiling. She shivered to see it, longing to touch the soft material, to feel it caressing her naked body.

Books were piled high on a table. They were bound with leather and she wondered if he'd used his magic to keep up with the outside world. It was said djinn knew many things, spoke all languages and could control the elements.

His head turned to the side and she got the briefest glance of his face. When he spoke, his voice was dark, low, predatory and powerful all at the same time. To hear it, she knew she'd found the right man. "Lucienne de la Rue. You have come to free me from this prison?"

"Yes," Lucienne whispered. Her own voice was husky with her passion.

"You come to me willingly?" he asked.

"Yes."

"You know that to free me from this prison, you must offer me your body to use as I will?" he insisted. Suddenly, his eyes lifted and he turned to look at her without really moving his feet. His hips angled and because of the way his arm fell at his side, the length and size of his cock was hidden from view. He had chiseled, hard features. His dark gaze swept over her form and she felt naked with only the thin linen of the ancient gown between them. "You must prove to me that you are worthy of freeing me."

Not as confident as before, she whispered, "Yes."

"Before I agree, I would have you tell me why." He was still partially turned from her, but from what she could see the tight muscles continued over his front.

Lucienne nodded. "My destiny has told me to come to you. I've searched for you. My family has searched for you ever since you were banished. I know that passion will free you from this prison."

"And I suppose you know that once I've had my fill, once I've been freed, I will become your slave for all eternity or until you grant me freedom," he answered. "I'll be bound to you, forced to grant your every desire, your every wish, no matter how depraved."

"Yes." This time she looked away. Her heart went out to him for the decision he faced. If he allowed her to free him, then he'd only be trading one prison for another. How was he to know that she'd be a kind mistress? How was he to know that what she'd demand of him wouldn't be worse than spending eternity alone in a buried cell? At least confined, he couldn't be forced to do harm. "It is my wish that you let me try to please you."

The djinni turned completely, standing before her as he lifted his arms to the side and said, "Then I agree. It will be as you wish."

Lucienne's jaw dropped. To say the man was well hung was an understatement. His cock was erect, protruding from his hips like a medieval battering ram ready to break through the castle gates. Only in this instance, her body was the castle and her pussy was the gates he'd be breaking through.

Even as she trembled in light of his nakedness, her body responded. It was all she could do to resist pulling up her skirt and jumping on top of him. Before she realized she'd even started walking, she was before him.

"Have you a name, djinni?" she asked, her gaze moving over his face and neck, down to his chest, wondering where she should start her temptations.

"Nadir."

His dark eyes bored into her and he didn't move to touch her as he waited to see what she would do. She knew that a frail woman might grow fearful of his hard, warrior body, of his severe look and daunting power. They might shy away from his turgid cock, so thick and tall as it pushed up from a bed of soft, dark hair.

Lucienne was not one of those women. She welcomed the power in him, had dreamt about it for so long. He was the reason mortal men had paled for her, could never satisfy her no matter how hard they tried. Mentally, she was prepared to be taken by him, to give herself in any way he wanted. Thinking that a man who'd spent centuries alone might have many decadent longings, only made her all the wetter.

Lucienne had to admit, the idea of this man being forced to fulfill every one of her desires for all eternity was very appealing. To be able to control his body, his hard cock into lifting to such fullness with just a command. To be whisked away whenever and she wherever wanted, to be fucked on demand and never be told no.

But first she had to please him. She glanced over his body once more. It was a very small price to pay to own such a treasure. Perhaps she wouldn't free him after he granted her wishes like she first planned. Perhaps, she'd keep him bound to her as her eternal love slave. When she'd vowed to free him completely, she'd never dreamt he'd look this delectable.

Lucienne reached behind her neck and unclasped the necklace, knowing men liked her breasts. They were large and soft with sensitive, dark nipples. As the jewelry slid off her body, so did the bodice of her gown. Her nipples contracted in the warm air, sending pure ecstatic pleasure down her stomach to settle between her tightening thighs. Nadir's his lips parted as he stared at her naked breasts and his breath came as harshly as hers.

She kicked off her sandals while pushing the linen from her hips. The warm air of the chamber surrounded her, but was nothing compared to the heat radiating from the man before her.

"Do you know how long it's been since I've seen a woman's body?" he asked.

"How about since you've felt a woman's body?" Lucienne leaned forward, rubbing her nipples lightly against his chest. His whole body tensed. Pleasure shot down from her breasts straight to her already aching loins. She felt the barest brush of his penis against her stomach as she leaned in to lightly lick his chest. "Or since you've felt a woman's lips on you?"

Nadir groaned.

Kissing him lightly, she began to kneel. Maybe if she sucked his cock, relieved some of the pressure inside him, it wouldn't be so daunting and big. The more she touched him, the more she wanted to. It was as if her body recognized him, knew it was meant to be with him on a primal level.

She'd never been so turned on her in life. The sexual energy he emitted—from his potent, masculine smell to the intense heat of his body—wrapped around her. She felt his power inside her, but also felt his loneliness and need. It added to her carnal hunger.

Lucienne's fingers skimmed his chest and hips. He had skin as smooth as silk and as hard as marble. She kissed his flat stomach, flicking her tongue over his navel. His taste was addictive, like warm chocolate. One lick wasn't enough.

This was so naughty of her and yet that was part of the appeal, part of what turned her on. Parting her lips, she kissed the thick head of his cock, letting it pass into her mouth. *Mmm*, his skin tasted just like chocolate—sweet, additive yet sugary.

Lucienne shivered. It was too good, she wanted more. She pulled his hips forward, thrusting his cock deep into her mouth so she could get a better taste. Nadir groaned and she felt his hands tangling in her long hair, pulling and pushing so that her head bobbed on his length. He was too big, not even fitting half way in as he nearly choked her with the thick mass.

Lucienne worked her hands over the extra length, instinctively knowing that such boldness would please him. What man, mortal or godlike, wouldn't want a naked woman kneeling before him sucking him dry? She cupped his balls, letting her finger hit the sensitive flesh just behind them. The erotic play of his stomach muscles rippled before her eyes as he pumped into her mouth. She sucked harder, wanting to taste his cum, wanting to discover if its flavor would match the sweet milk chocolate taste of his skin.

Nadir stiffened and jerked. His cock twitched in her mouth and his balls tightened in her palm. A hot jet of semen shot down her throat and she pulled back slightly to taste him.

Mmm, delicious.

The salty taste of his release was all potent male. She swallowed, eagerly taking in every drop, licking his dick clean. As she did so, she felt part of his spirit entering her. The beginning of a connection was formed. He was transferring control to her, control over him.

When she pulled her lips off and looked up at his face, his narrowed eyes were on her breasts. Lucienne boldly licked her lips. "Did that please you, djinni?"

"Yes, but it is not nearly enough. Already I have risen back to full strength."

Lucienne brought her gaze back to his cock. It was just as full and stiff as before she'd sucked it. So much for her theory on releasing pressure. The knowledge that he wanted more only excited her. She was ready to give him more.

Standing before him, she ran her hands onto her large breasts, rolling her nipples in her hands as he watched. "Sucking your cock has only made me want more, djinni. My pussy is ready—wet and hot and tight. It is my wish to fuck you with it."

A small smile curled the side of his mouth and appreciation lit his dark gaze. Nodding slightly, his long dark hair falling over his shoulders as me moved, he said, "As you wish."

Chapter Three
⁓

As you wish.

Lucienne almost orgasmed at the sound of those three short words. So much waiting, longing, planning, and now she was finally going to know what it was like to be taken by a djinni. She ran her hands down her stomach to her pussy, parting the wet folds as she stroked her clit. Already it was so wet with cream.

"How do you want me, Nadir?" she asked, breathless and eager. He didn't answer and she realized he wasn't going to help her out. It was up to her to lead him, to prove she was worthy of being his mistress. Taking his hand, she led him to the bed. She pulled the translucent gauze aside and he passed under the material only to lay on his back.

The gauze surrounded them, a seductive setting to their lovemaking. Lucienne crawled over him, surprised to see polished metal headboard above his head. Her own body reflected back to her—her swollen breasts, her large, dark nipples, the waves of her long, dark brown hair on her shoulders. She saw her round, blue eyes lined with black makeup. The thin trail of brown hair that guarded her pussy glistened with her body's cream.

Call it vanity but the sight of her own nakedness was turning her on more, as did the idea of being able to watch her body on his. She looked at Nadir, his hands folded behind his head. She caressed his chest, liking the texture of him beneath her palms. Her finger tangled in his dark locks, pushed at his erect nipples, hooked into his mouth to part his firm lips.

She was torn between watching her own reflection and looking at his gorgeous physique. His physique won. Taking his cock in both hands, she stroked him. There was no need—he was more than ready and so was she.

"When you belong to me, djinni, you will not just lay there," she promised him, working her wet, swollen clit against his penis. His eyes lit with passion, practically burning as they reflected his desire and she knew he was dying to touch her. "It will be my wish to have you touch me."

Lucienne lifted herself up and guided his cock to her pussy. She moaned loudly and rubbed him along her slit, wetting him with her cream. Sitting her weight down on him, she started to impale herself on his thick cock.

"Oh, oh," she cried. She'd never felt so full. Lucienne braced her hands on his chest, forced to ease him in slowly, but determined to take it all—every hot, thick inch. Her tight muscles squeezed him. She was no virgin, but he was stretching her like one.

Looking at the reflection, she saw she was almost there. With a stiff push, she seated him to the hilt. There was a moment of pain, but it only added to the sensation of pleasure that immediately followed. Nadir's eye widened as if surprised that she allowed him so deep.

"Oh yeah," she moaned boldly for him. Lucienne sat back and massaged her breasts, lifting her body slowly. "Do you feel how wet I am for you? How hot I am?"

"Yes," he growled, the muscles in his arms flexing as if to be free even as he kept them behind his head. He thrust his hips up, bracing his feet on the bed for leverage. "It pleases me that your body is so tight on my cock. But, it would please me more if you rode me hard. You said you wished to fuck me and I very much want to be fucked."

Lucienne panted, aroused by the sound of his voice and pleased by the fact he spoke of his desires. So he wanted it hard? Sounded good to her.

Slamming her body down on him, she began to ride, lifting and falling in hard thrusts. She used her thighs to control the movements as she pushed her hands through her hair. Her reflection stared back at her, wanton and beautiful. The pressure built inside her and she closed her eyes to bask in the feelings.

Then, to her surprise, she felt warm hands on her hips. Nadir was touching her, urging her on. He massaged her breasts, thumbed her clit and raised his body to meet her wild thrusts. Everywhere their skin touched was alive with his power and her passion. She felt him feeding off her desire and pleasure, giving her control over him in return. Soon, she would be the mistress and he her slave.

Lucienne came, crying out at the sudden force of her release. It had never felt this good before, so all-consuming. Nadir pinched her nipples and pulled them slightly, zipping a thread of pleasure through her, straight to her clit. She tensed, coming harder. Her muscles clamped him and he too cried out. It was the strangest sensation, but she could feel him filling her body with his seed. The connection grew stronger as he gave over more of himself.

Weakly, she fell against his chest. Her body was a little sore, but she didn't care. She'd waited her whole life for this feeling of completeness. The usual ache she felt after sex was gone as was the constant discontentment that nagged at her.

Falling on her side, she draped her limbs over his. Her hand found his chest, resting over his heart. It beat a steady rhythm and though he was breathing hard, the organ didn't pound like hers.

"I cannot believe that after so much time I might actually be free of this place," he said softly.

Lucienne looked at him, seeing the loneliness yet again. "The books on the nightstand."

"What about them?"

"They look new."

"They are," Nadir reached to touch her cheek. "I might be trapped, but down here I have my powers to keep me company. My kind craves knowledge, we hunger for it. The world has changed so much and I can watch that change through your books. I also see the changes in my mind, not all but a few."

"Is that how you knew my name?" she asked.

"I saw you," he admitted. "I've known about you for years. I called you to me, entered your head to whisper thoughts in to your ear."

Lucienne frowned. "What thoughts?"

"Wicked thoughts," he admitted. "My thoughts."

"You're the reason my body's been so..." Lucienne gasped.

"Insatiable?" he supplied, grinning wider. "Yes. I enjoyed watching you pleasure yourself as you looked for me. I gave you the wicked thoughts I had of you, so that I could pleasure myself as well. So many nights I fisted my cock, stroking it as you rode your own hand. But, it was never enough. I wanted your body on mine. I let your head fill with thoughts of me so you'd be ready to accept me when the time came, and you have."

"So, all those ideas? All those fantasies? Those were yours?" Lucienne let a slow smile curl her lips as she pushed up. Leaning on one arm, she skated her fingers over his chest.

"Yes," he said softly, closing his eyes as his hand drifted to caress her hip.

"The one where I'm being fucked on a flying carpet?" She quirked a brow.

"Yes. Modern perception of my kind is often amusing. I thought it fitting. Would you have preferred being stuck inside a magic lamp?"

Lucienne licked her lips. "How about the one where I'm bound and helpless and under your complete control?"

"A common djinni fantasy, I'm afraid. We are so controlled by others that many of us long to have our wishes fulfilled, our whims satisfied. Today, I will have a taste of that freedom. But soon I will belong to you completely and will be forced to bend to your every desire of me."

How sad. Lucienne took a deep breath, ashamed that she had thought to keep him as her sex slave.

Break him out of his prison first and then think of those things.

With that thought in mind, she pushed up. "And the one where I'm on my hands and knees before you, letting you fuck my ass?"

Nadir groaned. She watched his cock lift and form until it towered once more over his hips. His voice husky, he admitted, "I have thought of it often, yes."

Lucienne adjusted her hips, pushing up so she was on her hands and knees beside him on the bed. "It is my wish that you take me like that, djinni. I want you to be the first to fuck me in the ass."

Nadir groaned louder, nodding eagerly. His voice husky with desire, he said, "As you wish."

The unmistakable outline of a cock pressed into her ass, spreading her cheeks wide as Nadir parted her thighs from behind. His knees between hers kept her open to him. Lucienne tensed. After such an intense climax, her body needed a little coaxing. Nadir understood this without having to be told.

She moaned as he touched her. His hands explored the flesh of her back, touching her hips and thighs, stroking her neck. One hand snaked around her body, grabbing a breast firmly in his palm to tweak her nipple. The mound was big enough that it spilled over his fingers. Nadir made as sound of approval and soon he was leaning over her, stroking both breasts in his hands while gyrating his hips lightly against the cleft of her ass. Lucienne groaned, getting aroused all over again.

She pushed up, leaning her body against his and giving him better access to her chest. This was so much better when he was moving, touching, feeling. His hair tickled her breasts as he kissed her neck, nibbling lightly.

Lucienne watched in the headboard, liking the black streaks of his locks slashing across her breasts. His eyes met hers and he watched as well. She looked so pale when compared to him. His dark hands slid over her stomach, the fingers spread possessively over her as he pulled her tight to his body. He found her swollen clit and moaned as his fingers dipped into her hot juices.

"I like it better when you touch me," she admitted. "I love the feel of your hands."

Nadir sucked her earlobe into his mouth at the same time he thrust a thick finger inside her. To her amazement, cream flooded out of her body to coat his fingers in a hot wave as if he called her arousal forth. Gasping, she jerked her hips. He urged her down so she was again on all fours before him.

Lucienne tossed her hair back over her shoulder. Nadir's beautiful body was behind her. He again ran his fingers inside her channel, milking cream from her body. How could she be so wet? So needy? It was as if her body would never get enough. She thought about the future and all she saw was Nadir in her bed, touching her, fucking her, making love to her slowly. That was what she wanted. But if she granted him freedom, was that what she'd get? If she freed him, would he leave her?

The ache she felt in her chest was almost unbearable. If not for her heightened state of arousal, she'd have cried out in agony. Instead she cried out from the pleasure he wrought. How could another man ever satisfy her? She'd fantasized about Nadir for so long, felt connected to him, felt that connection growing with each brush of their skin. Was this the curse of the djinn? Once a mortal felt their power did nothing else matter? Is that why the djinn were rarely freed from service?

How could she let him go after this?

Lucienne licked her lips. Nadir continued to move behind her, touching her hips, kissing and biting the cheeks of her ass. After he took his time exploring her, he pulled back slightly. She felt his hands on her, gliding her cream over her already soaked pussy, drawing back to the tight rosette he found buried between her cheeks.

Nadir wet her ass with her own cream, milking it from her body so his cock would glide when he finally took her. His finger pressed inside, rimming her anus, stretching it. Lucienne cried out at the sheer pleasure of his probing. His large shaft pressed against her slit, stretching her slick channel again as he glided into her pussy. It felt so good, she pressed back for more.

"That's it," he moaned. He thrust a few times. "Get me good and wet."

"Ah no, not yet," she moaned in disappointment as he slipped his cock out of her. But, when he drew the thick tip up between her cheeks, she knew what he was doing.

His hand rubbed along her back as he whispered, "Relax."

Instantly, her muscles obeyed. He pressed forward, his cock gliding in the cream he'd called forth as he broke open her untried ass. Lucienne discovered nerves and sensations she didn't know her body had.

Panting, she let him have his way with her, trusting him with her body as he eased her open. It didn't hurt. His hand motioned over her back and stomach, taking away any discomfort and leaving only pure, mind-altering pleasure.

Lucienne spread her legs wider and sat herself back, seating him to the hilt. Nadir made raw and primitive noises, telling her how tight she was, how hot, how much he wanted to fuck her, how long he'd waited.

To know he'd longed for her as she longed for him drove her over the edge of reason. She cried out, begging him to take her hard. His large cock moved roughly inside her tight ass as he obeyed, pounding her fast and vigorously from behind. He'd prepared her well and she was slick and ready to be ridden. A finger dug into her wet folds, finding the sensitive pearl buried there.

Watching him take her, his face contorted with ecstasy, was too much. Her body cried out for release. A wicked smile came to his face and his eyes met hers in the reflection as he said, "Not yet."

Lucienne moaned, panted, begged, screamed. Nadir kept her on the brink of release, transfixed in that moment just before the tremors would overtake her. He growled, his muscled body like that of a god. His dark eyes flashed with fire and promise until his body seemed to glow with the power of what he was.

The glow surrounded her, spreading from him as it crawled over her skin. She was cold and hot all at the same time. Her nipples ached to the point they felt like they might burst. As the glow started to fade, Nadir let his control over her go. She orgasmed hard and long, trembling and clenching violently as he embedded himself deep in her ass.

Grunting, she felt his seed spilling inside her. The connection between them was complete. She'd pleased him with her forwardness and had given him passion and pleasure. Now, he was hers to command and control. Every whim would be fulfilled. Every desire met. Every need taken care of. She had her djinni.

Lucienne collapsed on the bed, taking long hard breaths as she recovered. Finally, when she turned over onto her back, she saw Nadir sitting at the end of the bed. Two thick, golden bracelets clasped around his wrists and two more, thinner ones around his upper arms. The bracelets that had graced her arms were gone.

A narrow band wrapped his forehead. It dipped down in the middle only to disappear beneath his dark hair. And to complete the picture, a pair of loose red pants were on his legs.

"You're mine now, aren't you?" she asked, studying her djinni in awe. Even now, bound as her slave, she found him irresistible and handsome.

Nadir bowed his head like a good servant, and said, "As you wish."

Chapter Four
ℬ

Lucienne saw the blank look on his face as he bowed, but wasn't fooled by it. There was a sadness to him now, but also an acceptance. His was a life of slavery and even though he had power, he didn't have the self-will to use it.

She knew she couldn't keep him forever. Lucienne wanted to desperately, but it wasn't right. Her goal in finding him had been to free him. If she didn't do at least that, she was no better than the men who put him here in the first place.

Just one time. One time as my slave to see what it's like and then I'll let him go.

"Nadir, I wish to feel rested and bathed," she said. "And I wish for you to feel the same."

He nodded, drawing his hands to the side as he bowed, "As you wish."

Instantly, she felt as if her body was freshly cleaned, scented with jasmine and rubbed with lotions. The tiredness of having sex three marvelous times, and days before that searching for him, went away.

"I'm hungry," she said. "I wish to eat."

"As you wish," he said, bowing to her again. A tray of fruit and cream appeared before her.

"Feed me," she said. He hesitated. "I wish for you to feed me."

"As you wish."

Nadir fed her, dipping the fruit in cream and lifting it to her mouth. He stared at her lips as she sucked his fingers into her mouth. Even as her slave, he still desired her. Afterward, she wished the tray away.

Eyeing his tight body, she lay back on the bed, still naked. "I wish for you to dance for me."

"As you wish." Music sounded, an ancient song. He disappeared from the bed, only to reappear on the other side of the translucent gauze. His hips thrust and moved in the most seductive way as he twirled around the room to entertain her with an ancient dance. His dark eyes met hers and she could see the stiff outline of his cock through his pants. He was enjoying her game as well.

Lucienne thought of all her fantasies. One time was all she was allowing herself as his mistress. Any more than that and it might be too hard to let go. Which fantasy should she pick? Then, grinning, she said, "Nadir, I wish for there to be two of you. Can you do that?"

Nadir bowed. She watched him. Behind her, she heard his voice say, "As you wish."

She gasped looking around to the other side of the bed. There were now two of him dancing for her. They came to the end of the bed, thrusting in rhythm to the music. Their hands reached out, parting the gauze so she could better see their delicious bodies undulating for her pleasure. Their arms brushed as they moved closer, a seductive show as each one caressed his own body. Her pussy was wet and both sets of eyes stared at her parted thighs. Two cocks bulged against pants. Lucienne knew she'd picked the perfect fantasy to fulfill—two djinn to pleasure her, two djinn completely focused on her. This would be an experience she would never forget.

"Come to me," she urged them. Even though she didn't wish it, they obeyed. They kept dancing, coming to their knees on the bed. Since they were both technically him, there was no jealousy in their eyes.

Lucienne touched her sex, stroking it as she watched them crawl slowly forward. She opened her mouth, accommodating her harsh breath. "I wish for you to be naked."

"As you wish," they said in unison. Instantly their pants were gone, but the jewelry remained. They continued forward, their bodies moving in perfect time with each other, each muscle flexing and contracting the exact same way on both of them.

She shuddered, eyeing the two cocks. "I want you both to take me."

As she said the word "both", Nadir grinned — both of him. It was a wickedly seductive look, holding much promise.

They stopped dancing but the music continued. She kneeled on the bed. One came up behind her, the other came in front of her. Four hands rubbed her flesh, squeezing and pinching the tender mounds of her breasts, dipping between her thighs to stir her passion to greater heights. Lucienne moaned, gasping at the mindless pleasure of being taken by two men.

Two mouths kissed her — sucking her breasts, biting and licking her sensitive ass cheeks. She'd never felt anything so erotically wicked, and yet so wonderfully right. Sensations flooded her from every direction. Everywhere she touched she found hard, muscled flesh. Rocking her hips back and forth, she tried to rub herself against their cocks only to become frustrated when both Nadirs teased her by pulling back.

It was almost too much. She cried out begging them for more, to end the torment they wrought between her thighs. Her pussy dripped with cream, throbbing to be filled. Then finally two hands reached for her, one from the front and one from behind, to press up into her aching pussy. She groaned a throaty sound of pure ecstasy as they both fingered her at the same time, slipping in and out of her channel, stretching her wide as they slid over her sweet spot.

Lucienne continued to mindlessly let her hands glide over mountains and valleys of hard male flesh. This had to be heaven, being worshiped by two male gods, both of them Nadir. Her body heated to a fever pitch. Her heart beat out of control. Gasping, she demanded, "I wish for you both to take me at the same time. Take me now!"

"As you wish," they murmured in a low husky tone. She shivered in response. Even their voices seemed to caress her skin.

Tight bodies pressed into her, trapping her between walls of hard flesh. She felt their cocks from both sides, finding her ass and her pussy with deft precision. There was no hesitance in them even as her stomach tensed in anticipation of their combined thrusts.

They lifted her to a standing position. The one in back supported her weight as the other lifted her legs up. The Nadir in front thrust his turgid cock into her pussy, groaning loudly. Lucienne screamed in pleasure at the suddenness of it as he pumped his hips in shallow thrusts. She wiggled her hips, braced against the man at her back. The idea that the Nadir holding her up would be watching as the other fucked her only excited her more.

The one behind her made a harsh sound as if torn between pleasure and pain. He growled, pushing her forward only to angle his cock head toward her body. The Nadir in front paused, embedded deep as his counterpart worked his cock along her sensitive rosette. The one behind thrust hard, filling her tight ass with his engorged penis. She was glad when she felt him slide easily as if he'd lubed himself for her.

For a moment they didn't move, keeping her filled in both holes, pressing their tight bodies to hers to hold her up. Just being impaled like this created such a pressure that she was content just to feel the fullness of them inside her.

The men had other ideas. The cock slid from her ass, only to thrust—pulling and pushing as the other had, inside her pussy. Hands tightened on her flesh, but she was beyond knowing which belonged to whom. As one Nadir pumped into her ass, the other held still, completely embedded in her quivering pussy.

She wanted to come, but it was as if they held her back from release. She pushed up, wanting them both to take her at once. They seemed to understand her need. One held her thighs as the other reached around to her breasts. They moved in unison, probably because they were of one mind. Each thrust was timed to perfection as they both pulled out and pushed in together. She writhed against them, panting and moaning as they took her.

Lucienne might be their mistress, but their rock-hard bodies had the power over her. Her mind centered on her lower body. She was so full, stretched to the brink.

Suddenly, the rhythm changed, growing faster and harder. One pulled while the other pushed. Nadir thrust into her pussy, only to pull out as the other Nadir pushed into her ass. Sensation overwhelmed her as they fucked her.

Pussy. Ass. Pussy. Ass.

They rocked her between the both of them, impaling her with each pounding thrust. Hands were everywhere—pinching, squeezing, soothing. It was too much. She cried out, coming so hard that cream ran down over her thighs. But still they moved, grunting like wild animals as they had their way with her.

Pussy. Ass. Pussy. Ass.

"Ah, ah, Nadir," she cried.

They didn't let up. She felt marked by them, her body forced to mold around their giant cocks. She continued to shake, coming hard, and yet they didn't stop the sensations. Her climax lasted a long time, her body plundered by the two cocks as Nadir gave her everything she'd asked for and more. She leaned back and a mouth kissed her breast. She didn't open her eyes as she let the pleasure have her.

"Too much," she whispered. "Ah! Ah! There. Like that."

Suddenly, they both stopped, grunting and jerking in unison as they came inside her. Fingers gripped her flesh, holding tight. Her body was weak and she was draped between them. Every part of her was relaxed and numbed. They laid her gently on the bed, coming to rest at either side of her. Two hands, one from each, cupped her breasts, kneading them gently. The contact felt good so she let them touch her.

Moaning, she knew she couldn't indulge for too much longer. She had to think, had to get all her wishes out of the way before she released him. Lucienne's heart broke and she didn't want to let him go. She might never feel like this again.

"I wish for you to become whole again," Lucienne said.

A hand disappeared, leaving one Nadir to answer, "As you wish."

Chapter Five
๛

Lucienne tried to think, but she fell asleep instead. She couldn't help it. Her body was so spent she couldn't keep her eyes open.

When she awoke, Nadir was sitting in his chair reading. The gauze hanging about the bed was parted so she could see him easily. He was again dressed in his loose red pants, but his chest was bare. She was covered with a soft fleece blanket and she knew he'd covered her up. His thoughtfulness touched her.

Sitting up, she yawned. Nadir instantly closed the book and stood before her as if waiting for her to command him. Lucienne would never be able to stand herself if she were to keep him, forcing him into slavery. It just wasn't right.

"I wish for the other djinn to be freed," Lucienne said. She hugged the blanket around her naked body.

"I can't do that, I'm sorry," he answered. "Only a mistress can free them."

"Then I wish for them to be moved from one prison to another. I wish for them to be set into the path of their true mistresses, the ones who can free them."

Nadir nodded, lifting his hands to the side. "As you wish."

"It's done? It worked?"

"Yes." He smiled slightly in what could only be gratitude. "It is as you wished. The djinn are being moved."

"Good," Lucienne sighed. "I suppose that is really all I can do for them."

"It is very generous, mistress," Nadir said. "It is more than most would think to do."

He stood proud and tall before her. It was very tempting to order him to fulfill her desires again. She resisted. Lucienne had her one fantasy and that would have to be enough. If he came to her again, it would be of his own free will. If he stayed, it would be for the same reason—because that's what *he* wanted.

"I wish to have money and good fortune. I wish for good heath, a nice home and fine things," Lucienne said.

"As you wish," he answered, his eyes dulling some. "But, I must warn you. These things alone cannot bring you happiness."

"I know," she answered, "but they will bring me comfort in never having to worry about such things as money."

He nodded.

"I wish for the same for my family," she said.

"As you wish."

"I wish for…" she hesitated. What else did she want? She had so much time to think about what she'd asked for and suddenly she couldn't think of them. It would be horrible to let him go only to discover she'd forgotten something important. But as she looked at him, all she could think about was wishing for him to stay with her forever. The idea of losing him hurt. Surely that was love, wasn't it? Every part of her felt him. Every part of her reached and longed for him. No matter how short a time she was in his presence, he'd been with her much longer than that.

"Love?" he asked as if reading her mind.

"No," Lucienne said, turning her gaze away from him. "That I do not wish for."

When she glanced at him, his head was tilted and his eyes were rounded in surprise.

"To wish for someone to love me would be pointless. It would not really be love if I had to wish for it, at least not the love I would have. I would have someone love freely. Only then would the emotion be pure. To force it would..." She shrugged. Forcing love would only make her lover her slave, not a man who freely loved a woman. She wanted to be chosen, not obeyed.

Nadir smiled and nodded.

Lucienne took a deep breath. Slowly lying back on the bed, she put her wrist together and lifted them to rest over her head. "I wish for you to bind me, Nadir. Bind me to the bed so I cannot escape until you free me."

He looked confused, but he bowed before her. "As you wish."

Her wrists were instantly secured over her head. Lucienne licked her lips. Was this crazy? Was she making a mistake? Once free, would he leave her tied to the bed?

"I have one more wish," she whispered, shaking in her nervousness.

"All you have to do is ask me and I will grant it," he said.

"I wish..." Lucienne took a deep breath, staring at him, watching his face. "I wish for you to be free of me and all others for all time. You should never have to be in another's service."

For a moment, he looked too stunned to move. He stared at her, his expression questioning. Very slowly, he bowed, and whispered, "As you wish, mistress."

Her body glowed and the control she had over him left her and flowed back into him. The shackles on his arms disappeared as did the crown around his head. He took a deep breath and then another, looking at his arms.

"I am free," he said. "Truly free."

"Yes," Lucienne added. "And I am bound for your pleasure. Only you can release me. You can choose to find your pleasure in me or leave me here to rot." She took a deep breath. "You can just leave me. Or you can choose to stay with me. Forever. The choice is yours. Your will is your own as is your future. Now, it is I whose future depends on your mood."

Nadir stared at her.

"What will you do with me, djinni? What will be my fate?" she asked. Every part of her waited for his answer.

"Why have you done this? Why put yourself in such a position? I could leave you here to starve. I could keep you alive, locked in this prison as I have been." He took a step closer to the bed where she lay bound. "Why put your fate in my hands?"

"To prove to you that I love you, Nadir," she whispered. "And to prove it to myself. It's crazy, I know. It makes no sense, but I have loved you for a long time. I've felt you, gave up everything to look for you. Now that I've found you, I have completed what I set out to do. I have freed you. If you stay with me, it will be because it pleases you to do so."

He waited so long to answer that she grew afraid she'd been wrong, that he might actually leave her. His dark eyes studied her, contemplating her for a long time.

"What is it you wish me to do, Lucienne?" he crawled onto the bed and sat next to her. His hand shook slightly as he pulled the blanket off her breasts. The fleece was a slow caress over her body as he bared it to his view. He tossed the blanket aside. They were suddenly cocooned in the gauzy prison as the material enclosed them once more. "Do you wish me to stay with you?"

"Yes," she gasped as his fingers slid up her calf to her inner thigh.

"Do you wish me to make love to you?" His voice was raw, attesting to his need. Her eyes roamed over his flesh, seeing the bulge beneath his red pants.

"Oh yes." She squirmed, parting her thighs for him. Automatically, she pulled her arms, wanting to reach for him, but they were trapped. "Please, yes."

"Will you beg me to?" He leaned over, his tongue extending from his mouth to lightly flick her nipple back and forth, swirling around it in slow circles. She arched her back trying to get her nipple closer but he merely teased her.

"Mmm, please, Nadir, please have your way with me. Make love to me, I beg you. I'll do anything." Lucienne trembled. There was something erotic and fulfilling about being under his complete control, subject to his every whim. He had unlimited powers, could do whatever he wanted to her body without consequence.

Something gripped her ankles and pulled. She looked down, seeing straps forcing her knees up and her legs apart. Nadir stared at her wet slit, licking his lips. When the pulling stopped, her legs were parted wide for him, exposing her sex.

"I've been longing to drink from you, but you did not ask for it," he admitted. His body moved with swift grace as his body blurred and drifted to kneel between her thighs. "Now I will have my fill."

His eyes met hers as he slowly lowered his mouth to her. Moaning loudly, he licked her, parting her folds with his warm tongue, the movement languid and slow as he savored her taste. Pulling his tongue back into his mouth, he licked his lips. "Delicious."

Her body answered that one, low word with a torrent of cream, flooding her already wet pussy. It was pure torture. He lay on his stomach, idly stroking her with his tongue, twirling her clit, dipping just beyond the opening of her sex. If he didn't latch down on her soon, she would surely die.

"Ah, Nadir, please," she begged.

He groaned, giving her body what it needed. A finger slipped into her channel, stroking the sweet spot he found inside. He kept a steady rhythm as his mouth closed over her clit, sucking her hard, nibbling her. She was trapped by the ties to her legs and wrists, but she managed to wiggle just enough to thoroughly enjoy the small orgasm he let her have.

It wasn't enough, though. She wanted more. After feeling the great release he was capable of giving her, the light tremors weren't enough.

"Please, Nadir."

"I like it when you beg for me," he growled, his dark eyes hot with fire. He sat back and his pants dissolved, leaving his body naked once more. His cock was just as big as when she'd first seen it, standing proud from his trim hips. Slowly, he fisted it with both hands, gripping his weapon as he watched her squirm to be free.

"Please, ah, please."

"Beg for my cock," he ordered.

"Yes," she moaned. "Please, give it to me."

He grinned, a dark look as straps again grew from the bed, slithering over her large breasts, crossing between them to hold her chest down. More straps covered her. They crossed her stomach, winding around her thighs like fingers, holding her legs wide.

The straps made her breasts stand tall, the nipples erect like two beacons eager for attention. Her sex wept for his cock and her nipples ached to be sucked. The straps tightened and released as she tried to move, a caress all its own.

"Nadir," she mindlessly pleaded. "Please, give it to me. Fuck me."

Nadir sat back between her thighs, looking over what he had created. He smiled in approval. His hands twisted his shaft from root to tip. Lucienne was forced to watch him, unable to take her eyes away from his hands on the distended flesh. He palmed his balls, rolling them. His body jerked and he kept masturbating, pleasuring himself as he forced her to watch.

A little bead of moisture gathered at the tip. She opened her mouth, wishing he'd let her taste him. But, this wasn't about her wishes, this was what he wanted. Knowing he got off on controlling her was exciting, for Lucienne was quickly discovering that she liked being controlled.

She waited for him to spray her body with his cum. Just the thought of it made her close to climax. The hot jets of it would caress her, covering her naked breasts and easing the tension she felt in them to be touched. He eased up, slowing his hands and denying her his seed.

"Please let me have your cock. I'll be a good girl. I'll do whatever you want." Lucienne cried out, frustrated at the intensity to which he aroused her.

"Say you'll stay with me," he commanded. "Give me your word that you will obey me, pleasure me as I would be pleasured. Do this and in return I will grant your every desire. We will belong to each other."

"Yes, a thousand times yes!" She panted. Lucienne meant it too. This was her destiny and there was no reason to fight it. Only he could please her. *"Please!"*

Nadir grinned, coming over her bound body. Her muscles clenched, ready to pull him in. She closed her eyes, tensing as she felt the first brush of his cock head probing her sex. And then he thrust, steady, sure, hard inside her aching pussy. His thick cock filled her and she nearly screamed at the tight fit of him.

Nadir pumped into her, taking her hard and strong, working his hips in small circles. His body moved over her bound one. Straps moved over her nipples, almost like a clamp. The sensation was too much. Her body tensed, spasming out of control as she came. He cried out, a rapturous sound of release as he came inside her body.

Lucienne's body was instantly freed the second his climax finished. She drew her arms down, moving to touch his shoulders. Her limbs were weak and even her bones were numb from the pleasure. Unable to hold them up, they dropped along her body. Nadir crawled to her side, wrapping her in his arms.

"You're amazing," he whispered, kissing her temple. "You pleased me the moment I first saw you."

"Mmm," she moaned, unable to speak just yet. She felt too good, too relaxed.

"Did you mean it when you said you love me?"

Lucienne looked at him, instantly melted by the hesitant look in his eyes. "Yes, I meant it. I do love you. Don't ask me to explain, I can't."

"I've been around enough to know love and I love you as well." Nadir kissed her temple, holding her close. "I want nothing more than to stay with you as your djinni, because I choose it and because you choose me."

Lucienne smiled, reaching to cup his handsome face. Slowly, she nodded in agreement. "As you wish."

Also by Michelle Pillow

About the Author

෨

Michelle M Pillow has always had an active imagination. Ever since she can remember, she's had a strange fascination with anything supernatural—ghosts, magical powers, and oh…vampires. What could be more alluring than being immortal, all-powerful, and eternally beautiful? After discovering historical romance novels in high school, it was only natural that the supernatural and romance elements should someday meet in her wonderland of a brain. She's glad they did, for their children have been pouring onto the computer screen ever since.

She is married (madly in love) and has a wonderful family.

Michelle would love to hear from you and tries to answer her emails in a timely fashion. That is if the current hero will let her go long enough to check the computer.

Michelle welcomes comments from readers. You can find her website and email address on her author bio page at www.ellorascave.com.

Tell Us What You Think

We appreciate hearing reader opinions about our books. You can email us at Comments@EllorasCave.com.

WEB OF DESIRE
Cathryn Fox

&

Prologue
&

As Ally Shears approached the old abandoned mansion she felt her stomach knot and her mouth go dry. She hated what she was about to do, but knew she had little choice in the matter. Mentally reciting the banishing spell from her Book of Charms, she reached into her jeans, her fingers connecting with the packet of herbs needed to send her cousin to the netherworld.

Dodging a low-hanging branch that fringed the walkway, she made her way down the narrow path leading to the decrepit house on Manor Drive. The soothing scent from a nearby lilac reached her nostrils but did little to ease her ragged nerves. With light footsteps, she crept up the stairs in search of Selina. Even though Ally hated the task before her, she knew it was best for the townsfolk. Banishing her cousin to the netherworld was a much better alternative than what the angry women of the town would likely do to Selina for using witchcraft on their beloved men.

If her cousin couldn't abide by the council's rules and use her witchcraft only for the betterment of mankind, then Ally had no choice but to take matters into her own hands.

The sleepy southern town of Belhaven had been charitable enough to take in their kind hundreds of years ago and keep their witchcraft a secret from the rest of the world. The least *they* could do was adhere to the laws set in place and behave like respectable citizens. And being a respectable citizen did *not* mean spinning a giant spider web to catch the town men and have your wicked way with them.

No matter how naughtily delicious that sounded.

Selina's wicked stunts had gained the town's attention and earned her a banishment spell. Ally insisted she be the one to cast it, for Selina's own safety. The truth was, the two were very close. Selina had been there on the worst night of Ally's life. Consoling her when Tanner Cage, the only man Ally had ever loved, stood her up on prom night and skipped town the next day. That closeness made the discovery of Selina's secret antics all the more shocking to Ally.

Ally pushed open the door and inched inside, fearing Selina would detect her presence and surmise her intentions before Ally had a chance to cast the spell. A moan sounded from the back bedroom, drawing her attention.

Ally followed the sound. She craned her neck and peered into the dimly lit room. What she saw frightened and intrigued her at the same time. Smack-dab in the middle of the room was a huge floor-to-ceiling web with a gorgeous, well-endowed man attached. Whacking a crop across her palm, Selina circled him, keeping a wide berth as she examined his rippled physique.

Selina turned at the sound of Ally moving into the room. She arched a delighted brow. "Hello, cousin. How nice of you to join me."

"I'm not here to *join* you, Selina."

"No?"

Fingering the packet in her pocket, Ally stepped closer. "You can't do this, Selina. It's wrong."

"Tsk…tsk…always the good witch, Ally." She slapped the crop harder against her palm and then pointed it at Ally. "I know deep inside there is a part of you that would love to have your very own toy like this." She waved her hand toward her naked captive. "Besides, look at that beast." She pointed to his erection. "He doesn't look too distraught to me."

Ally was pretty sure his girlfriend would be. "It's still wrong, Selina."

Selina chuckled. "Why don't you let your naughty little witch out to play once in a while?"

Ally grabbed the herbs from her pocket and sprinkled them in the air. A cloud of fog formed around Selina. Ally began to chant the banishing spell.

Selina's eyes opened wide. Her hands flew up in a halting motion. The crop fell to the floor. "Ally no," she cried, her voice growing faint as Ally circled her and continued to recite the spell.

Ally sprinkled more herbs into the air. "I'm sorry, Selina, you gave me no choice. Believe me, I'm doing this for your own good."

Selina's skin grew translucent. Her gaze locked on Ally's. "I'll be back, Ally. Just wait and see…"

Those were the last words Ally heard before her cousin disappeared into the fog.

Chapter One
Ten years later

ɛ)

Something was not right in the sleepy southern town of Belhaven.

Ally Shears placed a book on the gray metal shelf in front of her as a shiver of unease crawled over her skin like an insect. Every nerve ending in her body began tingling with foreboding and she knew—better than she knew every nook and cranny in the library she'd been working at for the past few years—that a dark cloud had descended over the town.

She felt a presence behind her. Ally spun around, half expecting to see her banished cousin hovering there. Instead, she gasped in surprise as the handsome Sheriff Devlin came charging forward. Startled by the anger in his eyes, she pressed a hand to her chest and took one small step backwards, positioning herself behind a rack of books.

"Selina's back in town," he growled, his dark eyes narrowing to mere slits as he fisted his broad hands at his sides.

She didn't care for his accusatory look. Did he somehow think this was her fault? After all, she had been the one to cast the banishing spell years previous. She schooled her expression. "Yes, I know," she said, keeping her voice low, controlled. She'd felt Selina's presence all day but had hoped like hell she'd been mistaken.

He drew an impatient breath and leaned toward her, using his height to look down on her. "She was spotted sneaking out of the old abandoned house on Manor Drive."

Ally frowned. Why they hadn't torn that decrepit old place down was beyond her. Especially after they'd found all of those men captured in Selina's silken webs. Men she'd lured to the manor and done sexual things to. Things that had left the town's women reeling, and some of the town men, well...violated. As a good, law-abiding witch, Ally would never consider doing something so wicked.

The sheriff raked an impatient hand through his thick black hair. "We need you to go over there, check things out and cast another banishment spell." He gave an angry shake of his head. "One that will hopefully *take* this time," he grumped, his dark brows furrowing slightly as he glared at her.

Ally wove her fingers together and resisted the urge to spin her own web and secure the sheriff to it. For punishment only. She never had cared for the way he looked down his nose at her since "the trouble" — as it had become known around town.

She pushed Devlin's remarks to the back of her mind. Right now she needed to concentrate on the herbs required for the spell to send Selina back to the netherworld, for the good of the town as well as Selina. Ally certainly didn't want her cousin taunting and tormenting the decent people returning to Belhaven for their high-school reunion this week — the same people who had rightfully demanded her banishment in the first place.

Centuries ago, Ally's descendants had escaped the Salem witch trials and settled in the scarcely populated, sleepy little town of Belhaven, a place outsiders rarely visited. When word eventually leaked that they were witches, the townsfolk were prepared to burn them at the stake. But after proving that they had healing powers and were able to cure the sick and help the wounded, the city council had allowed the witches to stay, and swore to keep them secret from the rest of the world, providing they followed very stringent rules and only used their craft for the good of the people.

They lived amongst the townsfolk for centuries, gaining respect and trust. Of course, during Ally's lifetime, witchcraft had become much more accepted, as Wicca was practiced by many throughout the world.

Life had been pleasant in their small community—until Selina decided to wield power for her own selfish needs. It became evident that she had an agenda of her own when she began breaking every rule put in place by the council. Spinning strong, sticky webs made from fine, silky threads, she captured the good men of Belhaven and used them for her own pleasure. Now Ally and the rest of her clan were suffering the repercussions of her cousin's self-indulgent acts. The council had hushed up the incident, knowing that, with the exception of Selina, the witches were all law-abiding folks. Unfortunately, many no longer trusted them, going out of their way to avoid her kind.

Ally took a quick peek at her watch and noted it was nearing four o' clock. Deciding to check out early, she glanced at Devlin. "I'm closing up now. I'll head over there just as soon as I lock the door and gather some herbs for the spell." She tilted her head to look him in the eye. "Will you be accompanying me?" she asked with bright-eyed innocence, knowing full well that the thought of going inside the mansion made the sheriff shiver beneath his wide-brimmed hat.

Her smile stretched wickedly as she watched him squirm under her steady gaze. His jaw clenched. "You think you'll need me?" he asked in an unstable voice. Before he drove his hands into his front pockets she noticed them shake.

She shrugged. "I might. Of course, if you're afraid…"

He gave a quick shake of his head. His eyes flashed. "It's not that—"

Cutting him off, she folded her arms across her chest. "Well, what exactly is it then?" she asked, deadpan.

"I think I should keep watch from outside. To wait for Selina's return." His deep voice stammered.

When she smirked at him he blurted out, "I'm *not* afraid."

Well, he should be afraid, Ally mused, *because Selina had certainly had it out for him ever since he'd flatly turned her down, years ago. Lord knows what her cousin would do to him, given the opportunity. The last place Devlin wanted to be caught was in one of Selina's webs.*

Or *hers*, for that matter, if she ever decided to spin one.

Lucky for the town, Ally was a good witch.

Chapter Two
ဆာ

Ally stood back and examined the crumbling mansion left abandoned for years. Ivy vines climbed the walls like snakes and coiled around the posts that supported the veranda. The grounds and walkway were overgrown with shrubs, weeds and wildflowers. With the sheriff remaining a good twenty feet behind her, she made her way onto the porch. Chips of old white paint peeled beneath her hand as she brushed her fingertips over the wooden railing leading up the steps.

When she reached the massive front entrance, she closed her fingers over the brass doorknob and pushed. The heavy door creaked open, the hinges moaning like a wounded animal. Ally looked over her shoulder and gave a curt nod to the sheriff, signaling she was going in.

She felt a sense of déjà vu as she squeezed the packet of herbs inside the front pocket of her jeans and took a tentative step inside the old house. The planked floorboards groaned beneath her. Every light footstep stirred the air. Small particles of dust rained down from the ceiling, dancing and shimmering in the long column of late afternoon sunlight that sliced through cracks in the decaying cedar siding.

The air smelled stale and pungent. Like day-old pizza and beer. Or socks that had been left in a gym bag too long. Ally crinkled her nose and concentrated on breathing through her mouth.

A murmur coming from the back of the mansion drew her attention. She quietly padded down the long, dark hallway until she stood outside a closed door. Pressing her ear to the wooden slats, she listened.

Silence.

She lowered herself onto her knees and peeked through the large keyhole. The sunshine slanting through the open window gave off sufficient light for her to see a man squirming, trying to break free from the strong, binding web that held him captive.

From ceiling to floor, a web had been spun in the center of the room. With his back clinging to the sticky strands, his hands were secured over his head. His long legs were spread wide apart and securely attached as well. With his head turned away from her, she couldn't discern his features. God, he was so big, like a Viking warrior. His presence swallowed up the small room.

She bit down on her bottom lip as she slowly perused the length of him. His thick, sculpted muscles bulged in all the right places and threatened to rip the seams of his snug jeans and short-sleeved shirt. She was actually quite surprised to find him still fully clothed. Selina obviously hadn't finished what she'd started.

Her gaze traveled over his unruly mass of dark hair and then lower, over his broad shoulders and tight abs, stopping only when she reached the apex of his legs. She swallowed hard. Oh *yes*, his muscles definitely bulged in all the right places. Whoever said good things come in small packages certainly wasn't talking about this guy. She stared at his impressive size for an endless moment as she undressed him with her eyes. Awareness started at her core and rippled onward and outward. Her whole body began tingling in the most interesting places. When she gave a sexy moan, he began to turn in her direction. As if she'd been caught with her hand in the cookie jar, Ally quickly pulled back from the keyhole and straightened. She brushed the dirt from her knees and took a fueling breath of courage before entering. She had no idea what else she was going to find behind that door.

When she closed her hand over the knob, a breeze from the open window stirred the air. Suddenly, a very enticing, very *familiar* smell seeped through the keyhole and reached her nostrils. She inhaled deeply as the spicy, manly scent sent her thoughts spiraling back in time.

Memories flashed through her mind like lightning. Memories of her senior prom and the handsome Tanner Cage, high-school heartthrob and captain of the football team.

She'd been so madly in love with him. She'd taken extra care in her appearance that beautiful spring evening, arranging her long golden curls on top of her head, letting a few tendrils spill down her neck, just the way he'd liked. Underneath her pale blue satin gown she wore a silky white chemise, knowing she was finally going to give her virginity to the man she loved.

The truth was, Ally had always loved Tanner. Since kindergarten, really. It wasn't until high school—when she'd traded her thick glasses for contacts, lost the braces and gotten curves in all the right places—that he'd begun to see her as something more than the neighborhood tomboy.

Tanner had asked her out during their senior year. After that first date, they became inseparable, joined at the lips, as some would say. They'd eagerly—and naïvely—talked about marriage.

A smiled touched Ally's mouth as she recalled his pet name for her. Ally Cat.

Tanner Cage had been her soul mate. Her everything. And she had been ready to take their relationship to the next level. They both wanted their first night together to be special and had agreed they would consummate their love on prom night. That night had never happened. He'd left her standing on her doorstep waiting for him. Ally had cried until the sun came up. The next day she heard Tanner skipped town and joined the military. Ally had never set eyes on him again and the last she heard he was doing an overseas tour of duty as a Navy SEAL.

Selina had stayed by her side, comforting her. Even though Selina had done wrong by the townsfolk, she'd always been there for Ally. They were family—blood sisters—which made it twice as difficult for Ally to banish her. But Ally knew the banishment was for Selina's own safety.

Tanner Cage had broken her heart and destroyed her belief in happily ever after. She'd been with other men since that dreadful night, of course, but how could she ever connect with a man emotionally? How could she ever find true love or give her heart to another when it belonged to one man—a man who didn't want it.

She shook her head, clearing away her painful thoughts. She gave a heavy sigh, knowing that if she ever did set eyes on him again, she'd make him pay for that dreadful night. He'd be smart to spend his life steering clear of her. She knew the well-disciplined witch inside her was only so forgiving.

She twisted the knob, eased the door open and stepped inside the room. Her eyes widened in astonishment as she took in the vision before her. The sound of her indrawn breath filled the air. Her pulse drummed in her neck and she had to lock her knees to avoid collapsing. Faltering backwards, she gripped the doorknob as if it were a lifeline.

When those beautiful, familiar green eyes met her gaze, the edges of her vision became fuzzy. Feeling lightheaded, she drew air into her lungs.

God, it couldn't be him. It just couldn't. Not after all this time.

His dark brows knitted together. "What do you want with me?" he asked, tugging hard on the binding threads. And what the fuck is this thing I'm stuck to?"

Ally bit down on her lip. The truth was, he was better off not knowing.

When she didn't answer, he asked again, "What do you want with me?"

She remembered that deep voice. So rich and enticing. Like warm, melted butter. It seeped into her skin and filled her with heated memories of his passionate touch, his fiery kisses.

Heat curled inside her. She pinched her lips tight and suppressed a ragged moan.

Was it really him or was she just dreaming? Had that delectable, familiar male scent simply caused her mind to conjure up the image?

She narrowed her gaze. "Tanner?" she asked quizzically, seeking verification that the man from her past had suddenly resurfaced.

He glared at her, confusion obvious in his gaze. "Do I know you?"

She drew in a sharp breath. It *was* him. And he didn't remember her. She straightened her spine and swallowed. Perhaps he couldn't see her well in the dark shadows of the room. She took a tentative step closer, providing him with a better view of her face.

"It's me. Ally."

"Ally?" He paused as though searching his memory. "I don't know anyone by the name of Ally."

Her heart crumbled like the burnt toast she'd eaten for breakfast. How could he not remember her? They'd been in *love*. At least she had thought they were. Was she so forgettable that the man she'd wanted to spend the rest of her life with could so easily dismissed her from his memories?

Determined to get to the bottom of it, Ally searched for an explanation. "Do you have amnesia? Or memory loss? Did something happen during your last tour of duty?"

"No," he bit out. "You obviously have me mixed up with someone else."

Another thought struck her and made her stomach curdle. Had somebody played with his memory? Used witchcraft on him? The only one she knew who had ever abused the craft was...Selina.

She opened her mouth to ask, but shut it when he cut her off with a glare. She *had* to be mistaken. Selina and Ally had been more like sisters than cousins. She recalled the way Selina had spent the night comforting her when Tanner had run off. Ally refused to believe Selina would hurt her like this. Besides, Selina's wicked antics hadn't started until a few years after Tanner had left town.

Hadn't they?

"Are you going to let me down?" he asked.

"I *was* going to," she replied, walking over to the table beside him to look over the contents. Lubricant, a pink vibrator, nipple clamps, two long candlesticks and a book of matches. A leather crop drew her attention. How interesting. She picked it up and ran her hands over the long, textured length of it. She wondered what kind of fun Selina'd had with that particular prop.

His body stiffened with annoyance. "What do you mean, you were going to?" he bit out.

Silence ensued as she took a long moment to peruse the captive man before her. Gone was the thin teenage boy she'd fallen for. In his place was a man. A man with broad shoulders and thick, sculpted muscles. A man who oozed sexuality in a way the young, high-school boy never had.

"You know, Tanner, you owe me something." She stepped close—close enough that his scent overwhelmed her senses. Pressing the crop against his cheek, she let it slide over his neck, his chest and lower until it grazed the huge bulge between his legs.

He flinched. His eyes darkened as disbelief marred his features. "How can I owe you anything? I don't even *know* you."

"That's where you're wrong. We knew each other quite...intimately," she murmured.

She watched his glance leave her face and wander down her body. He dragged his teeth over his bottom lip as his eyes latched upon her breasts. Ally felt her nipples harden involuntarily under his lusty gaze. Her chest heaved as a surge of blood rushed through her veins.

"Ally…" He let her name roll off his tongue as though he were testing it, tasting it. His gaze smoldered as it locked with hers. "If I'd known you…*intimately*," he said, lowering his voice, "there's no way in hell that I'd forget."

His warm breath caressed her face like a lover's kiss. Her body came alive, stimulated by his bold words. A tingle worked its way down her spine. She blinked and fought to recover her voice. "Well, it seems you did, now doesn't it?" she challenged.

He gave her a sexy, predatory grin. "Why don't you let me down and give me a chance to sample that hot body of yours. Perhaps that will help trigger my memory." His voice dripped with sensual promise.

She slowly walked around him, dragging the long crop over his hard body. She felt his muscles bunch. She stopped directly in front of him and looked deep into his gorgeous eyes. A sudden surge of anger and hurt welled up inside her. "Or perhaps I could leave you here and make you pay for forgetting me."

He growled and struggled with the silken web. "You wouldn't!" His voice sounded whiskey-rough.

When their gazes met and locked she expected to see rage. What she saw instead captivated her. Heat coiled deep in her belly as moisture gathered between her thighs. The passion that shimmered in his eyes made her breath catch and her anger recede. Her brain stalled and she had to remind herself to breathe.

"What exactly is it I *owe* you, Ally?" The deep timbre of his voice made her shudder.

"A prom night," she said and pressed the crop hard against his growing cock.

* * * * *

Tanner groaned and pressed into her touch. Fuck, that felt good. He had no idea who this woman was or what she thought he owed her, but if she kept touching him like that he was going to rupture an artery.

He though back to his senior year and couldn't recall ever knowing an Ally. He wasn't sure why she had brought up the prom. He'd never even gone. Never planned to. He'd always thought of it as a senseless ritual. Instead, he had met up with the guys, knocked back a few beers and then left town to join the military.

Ally reached out and swept aside a lock of his hair. When she did, he watched color bloom high on her cheeks and wondered what she was thinking. Wondered what the hell she planned on doing with that whip she clutched in her tightly fisted hand.

His question was quickly answered when Ally drove the crop between his jean-clad legs and pressed the knobbed end between his ass cheeks. It stung, but he liked it. He bit down on his bottom lip and forced himself not to show his reaction. *Holy shit.* He could hardly believe how turned on he was. When his eyes locked with hers, he was both aroused and chilled from the intensity in her gaze.

If he'd had a sexy woman like her waiting for him at the prom, no way in hell would he have ever skipped town.

With a featherlight touch she skimmed her fingers over his cheek, his lips and lower, until her hand hovered over the top button of his shirt. The feeling was erotically stimulating and every muscle in his body twitched. His heart began to pound beneath her touch.

Once again he racked his memory, trying to recall who she was. Nothing. Surely she was mistaken. Surely he didn't know her. His gaze traveled over her face. She was beautiful—exquisite, really—with honey-amber eyes and hair the soft golden color of a wheat field. Her full breasts narrowed to a slim waist that bloomed into curvy hips. Her long sexy legs were wrapped in a pair of snug-fitting jeans. And she smelled so damn good. Like vine-ripened raspberries. Her feminine aroma was vaguely familiar, yet he couldn't quite put his finger on it. He inhaled deeply, letting her scent fill his senses.

He shook his head. There was no way he'd ever forget a woman as sexy as she was. No way in hell. *Especially* if they'd been intimate.

When his gaze settled back on the creamy swell of her heavy breasts a tremor ripped through him. His mouth watered for a taste as his cock throbbed in response. He became acutely aware of how much his body ached for her touch.

She reacted to the tremor she felt in his body. Her fingers slipped from his chest and dropped to his cock. She cradled his erection in her delicate hand.

"Seems you might be a bit intrigued by my plan." Her sexy voice vibrated all the way down to his toes.

He swallowed and focused on what she was doing with her fingers. "What exactly *is* your plan?"

She gave him a sly smile. "If I told you, that would take the fun out of it, now wouldn't it?" When she gently squeezed his balls, he growled and thrust his hips forward. Unfortunately, the silky web prohibited him from moving too far.

"Let's just say I think you need to be punished for breaking my heart and abandoning me on prom night. I missed out on a night of lovemaking with you that I'd been dreaming about all year." Mischief danced in her eyes.

"Let me down from here, Ally," he growled. "I mean it." When she ignored his protests he continued, "If you don't, you'll pay." Perspiration beaded his forehead.

She shook her head slowly. Her eyebrows raised a fraction. "No, I don't think so. I kind of like you this way." She began working the buttons on his shirt. "Besides, you're the one who's going to pay."

The determined look in her eyes heated his body. A tremor moved through him — from passion, not anger.

"I could yell for help." He twisted his right hand and was surprised to find he'd somehow managed to snap the seemingly unbreakable silken bindings. He hid that information from her.

"Yes, I suppose you could." Her voice was a hoarse whisper. She met his gaze straight on and moistened her lips. "If you wanted to," she challenged. The heat in her eyes licked over his body.

Giving up on the buttons, she grabbed his shirt and ripped it open. The buttons popped and sprinkled on the floor. She splayed her hands over his chest and leaned in until her mouth was a breath away from his. Her fingers toyed with his nipples. He sucked in a sharp breath and exhaled a groan.

She pitched her voice low. "Do you want to scream, Tanner?" There was a little erotic whimper in the back of her throat.

He clenched his jaw. Yes. No. *Fuck.* How could he possibly make a rational decision when all the blood was draining from his head and settling low in his groin?

She brushed her mouth lightly over his. Her hips bumped into his thighs. Her puckered nipples pressed into his chest. A tremor racked his body. He growled, pressed his lips hungrily into her sweetness and deepened the kiss with wild abandon. The heat from her mouth scorched his soul and stirred the fire inside him. Blood pounded through his veins. Needing to touch her, he struggled against the silky web. She tasted like sex and sin and heaven, all at the same time.

Suddenly he knew there was no way in hell he was going to yell for help.

Chapter Three

Ally stepped back and took a moment to regroup. Her simple plan to arouse Tanner, leaving him unfulfilled and longing for more, the same way he'd left her many years ago, had suddenly become a little more complicated. His erotic kiss fueled her hunger and left her yearning for one of more substance. He was so beautiful, so muscular and so hard that her body came alive, just from at looking him.

The heat and energy radiating from his flesh stirred her libido. Warmth pooled in her pussy and filled her with a restless ache—an ache to feel skin against skin, to be kissed by his sensual lips, to be touched by his thick, capable hands, and to feel his growing erection stoke the fire simmering inside her.

Without realizing what she was doing, she cupped her breasts, ran her thumbs over her protruding nipples and whimpered. Her eyes connected with Tanner's. The look on his face told her all she needed to know. Watching her pleasure herself excited him. She bit down on her bottom lip and considered that bit of information. Perhaps that could be part of her plan. To let him watch as she touched herself. To leave him hot and needy while she eased the mounting tension deep inside her slick pussy.

"Do you like this, Tanner?" Ally ran her fingers down her neck and dipped them under the thin fabric of her T-shirt. A shiver prowled through her body and turned her inside out as his burning eyes left her face and lingered on her breasts. Throwing her head back, she moaned in delight as her warm fingers connected with her tight peaks. A fever rose in her and she knew she had to find release before her entire body went up in flames.

"Let me fuck you, Ally," he murmured, the rough timbre in his voice giving way to soft persuasion.

She looked him square in the eye. They were dark, full of lust. She sucked in a tight breath as her head began spinning. So tempting. So very, very tempting. She became hyperaware of the thick bulge between his legs. Her pussy moistened, urging her to give in to her desires. As much as she loved that idea, she knew that wasn't part of her plan. That would give *him* pleasure. Shaking her head to clear it, she fought her traitorous libido, reminding herself what he'd done to her.

Blowing out a shaky breath, she tried to keep the longing from her voice. "Why do I need you to fuck me, when I have this?" She walked over to the table and picked up the long, pink vibrator.

His nostrils flared. "Because my tongue can do things to you that that device can't."

For a brief moment she pictured his mouth buried deep inside the dark triangular patch at the apex of her legs. His tongue licking, sucking, nibbling, bringing her to previously undiscovered heights of ecstasy. Her whole body quivered as liquid desire dampened her panties.

She fought to find her voice. "Pretty sure of yourself, aren't you?"

"Yes," he growled with a touch of arrogance in his voice. "Let me down from here and I'll prove it."

When she shook her head back and forth he let out a roar of frustration. Dropping the rubber cock back on the table, she closed the distance between them. She ran her hand down his smooth, tanned chest. His moist skin felt wonderful beneath her fingers. Her hand dropped to his waistband. She unfastened his button and listened to the hiss of his zipper as she drew it down. "Just to show you that I'm not totally insensitive, I thought I'd give your cock some breathing room. It does seem rather constrained behind your tight jeans."

After she freed his erection, it sprang out from its restrictive confines, clamoring for attention. Ally gasped in surprise as her pulse leapt in her throat. He was so big, so thick. The swollen purple head looked velvety soft. Her fingers tingled, anticipating a touch. Her mouth watered for a taste. Desire burned so hot in her she felt dazed. The need to touch him, to stroke her tongue over his smoothness consumed her.

Raw, primitive urges took over, and before she realized what she was doing, she dropped to her knees. She moaned and pulled his cock into her hungry mouth.

She threaded her fingers through his silky curls and cupped his heavy balls. Rocking on her heels, she pumped his cock in and out of her slick mouth. She remained nestled between his legs for a long moment, her tongue stroking and laving his engorged shaft. Lust spread like wildfire through her body as she reveled in his taste.

His low growl of pleasure brought a smile to her face. It was easy to tell he was close to erupting. Her tongue urged him on. His balls tightened against his skin, his cock swelled in her mouth, liquid desire dripping from the tip. She pulled away, leaving him teetering on the edge.

"Don't stop, Ally. Please, not yet." His voice was harsh, rough. He thrust his hips forward in search of her mouth.

Ally stood on wobbly legs and met his gaze. She pouted her full lips. "It seems I've gone and wet my panties," she murmured.

He began panting heavily as she backed away and unsnapped her jeans.

She shook her hair from her face and presented him with a mischievous smile. "Perhaps I should take them off."

The heat in his eyes licked over her skin. "Yes, take them off. Take *everything* off," he blurted out as he struggled to free himself. "Let me see your cunt, Ally."

Ally seductively wiggled her backside as she slowly drew her pants over her thighs. Tanner's tortured curses reached her ears. "Fuck, Ally, what are you doing to me?"

She kicked her pants away and widened her legs. Desire twisted her insides as she dipped her finger inside her drenched panties. She drew in a tight breath as her nail grazed her inflamed clit. "Mmmmm..." she moaned, throwing her head back as she pleasured herself.

"I'm gonna fuck you if it's the last thing I do." His voice was a ragged whisper.

Ally paused and looked at him. His gorgeous green eyes were dark with heat — and promise.

"You can bet on it," he assured her. She bit down on her lip as a fine tingle of anticipation worked its way down her spine.

"Are you forgetting who's in control here?" She reached down and picked up the bright pink sex toy. Her eyes never once breaking the steamy hold she had on him as she stroked her hand over the bulbous head. She drew it into her mouth and licked the tip, imagining it was his cock she was suckling.

Tanner's eyes tracked her every movement. His visual caress did mysterious things to her nerve endings. His nostrils flared as he clenched his jaw. She watched with heated interest as his chest rose and fell in a fast, erratic pattern.

Keeping her gaze locked on his, Ally took small steps, widening the distance between them, until her back was pressed against the wall. Drawing her panties down she tossed them toward Tanner. They landed silently at his feet. Tanner's gaze dropped to her cunt. She positioned the rubber cock between her legs and opened her dewy folds, displaying the pink satiny skin of her most private flesh. "Is this what you wanted to see, Tanner?"

He gave a slow nod of his head and swallowed hard.

"You know—you could have had this on prom night if you hadn't run off," she murmured, lifting one leg and resting it on a nearby chair.

Tanner's jaw went slack, his eyes smoldering, and he was breathing as though he'd just run a marathon. He mumbled curses under his breath as he struggled to free himself.

In one smooth motion she breached her slick opening. The pink toy pushed against the walls of her tight pussy. She let out a long moan of pleasure as she savored the sensation. She slid the vibrator all the way into her slick core and back out again. Her liquid heat dripped over the rubbery head. All sense of time and place was lost on her as she worked the toy in and out of her heated channel and stroked her breasts with her other hand.

Blocking her mind to her audience of one, and concentrating only on her own pleasure, she pinched her eyes tight as she drove the thick rubber cock back inside her slick cunt. She was close, so close to finding release. Her breath came in ragged bursts as her orgasm neared.

"You're so sexy, baby." A rich, decadent rumble of pleasure sounded from the depths of his throat.

She loved the tone of his voice. So deep, so masculine. It seeped into her skin and filled her with a fiery need. She inhaled. His warm, masculine scent curled around her and urged her on. She pumped faster, harder until she heard the dark whisper of his voice again. He sounded close. So close, in fact, she thought she felt his hot breath on her cheek. But that was impossible. He was trapped in Selina's web.

Her lids flew open. She'd been so lost in sensation, she hadn't realized Tanner had freed himself. She took a quick moment to appraise the situation, then made a move to run.

Using his body weight, he pinned her against the wall. She could feel his cock pressing against her midriff. "I'm about to make good on my promise," he breathed into her ear, his hands tracing the pattern of her curves. She shivered under his seductive touch.

She opened her mouth, but before she could say anything he closed his lips over hers. He moved his hand to the small of her back and drew her pelvis closer to him. He pulled the rubber cock from her pussy and tossed it aside. "You won't need that anymore," he growled into her mouth. He parted her swollen folds and eased three thick fingers deep inside her cunt while his thumb scraped over her clit.

Ally could barely summon the strength to remain standing. She sagged against him and he tightened his hold, bracing her to him. His gaze locked on hers as he worked her into a state of aroused euphoria. She wanted to push him away and run, but she couldn't. It felt too good, too right.

His lips greedily closed over hers and branded her with his heat. Twining her arms around his neck, she began panting heavily. He expertly fucked her with his fingers until she was on the brink of a powerful orgasm. She felt almost desperate for release. The desire in his eyes sent shivers through her body.

"Take your shirt off," he ordered. In one fluid motion she peeled it over her head and tossed it aside.

When his hungry gaze settled on her milky cleavage, her pussy began to clench. "That's it, baby. Let me finish what you started." She fell under the spell of his deep, mesmerizing voice.

Craving the feel of his skin, she pulled him against her naked flesh and began rocking her hips, meeting and welcoming his every thrust. She ran her hands over his thick, corded muscles, reveling in the feel of his moist flesh.

"Let me show you what my tongue can do." His voice thinned to a whisper.

She opened her mouth to speak but no words formed. His burning eyes left her face as he slowly tracked down her body. Settling himself between her legs, he urged her thighs wide open and lowered his head. She shivered with delight at the touch of his soft, velvety tongue.

"Sweet Jesus, Tanner!" she cried and arched her spine.

She moved against him restlessly and plowed her fingers through his hair. The pleasure he was giving her was beyond her wildest imagination. He did things to her body that no one had ever done before. Things that made her dizzy, wild, feverish. She wanted to touch him. Everywhere. She wanted her mouth on his chest, his abdomen, his cock. It was too much, too intense.

Scraping her nails over his shoulders she pulled on him. "Stop...stop...God, don't stop," she begged, as he continued his mind-blowing erotic assault.

His tongue probed her soaked opening then licked her all the way from front to back. A jolt of fire curled around her and she began to quake. In no time at all an explosion tore through her as she shuddered her surrender.

Tanner let out a low growl of satisfaction when her juices poured into his mouth. Wrapping his arms around her waist, he held her and absorbed her tremors as she took her time coming back down to Earth. After her breathing regulated he slid up her body until his mouth hovered over hers.

Her heart lurched in her chest as she watched him. Every old feeling she had for him came clawing back to the surface. She was still so deeply in love with him. But her emotions were quickly squelched when she recalled that he didn't even remember who she was.

"Now wasn't that better than some toy?" he asked, his lips glistening with her desire. She could smell her heady scent on his breath.

Lowering her gaze to shadow the emotions in her eyes, she nodded. It occurred to her that the reason she'd kept him secured to the web wasn't to make him pay for leaving her—it was with the hope that he'd remember her, remember their past.

When he shifted closer, she felt the wet tip of his arousal press against her. She began to feel guilty for trying to keep him captive. Especially after he'd freed himself and given her such intense pleasure without taking anything for himself.

"I'm sorry," she murmured. "It was wrong of me to keep you captive. Let me make it up to you."

He pulled her into his embrace, twisted them around and began to walk her backwards. "What exactly do you have in mind?" he asked, a playful glint in his eyes.

She shrugged and nibbled on her lower lip. "I don't know. Maybe dinner."

He chuckled softly. "I have a better idea." His deep voice dropped to a whisper that caressed her body.

"Oh? And what would that be?" she asked tentatively, watching his thick muscles shift with each movement.

"Tell me more about this prom night we missed. What was so special about it? What were we going to do?" A warm smile turned up the corners of his sexy mouth and softened his features.

When she lowered her head, he cupped her chin and tilted her face until their eyes locked. "Tell me," he coaxed softly.

The tenderness in his voice made her blurt out the truth. "We...we were going to make love. You were going to be my first."

Wrapping his arms around her waist, he effortlessly picked her up and pushed her shoulder blades against the sticky web, trapping her.

Her eyes opened wide in surprise as the strong bindings secured her in place. "What...what are you doing?" she cried, alarm obvious in the tone of her voice. She felt her face go pale as she hopelessly struggled to free herself.

He picked up the leather crop and looked deep into her eyes.

"I'm going to give you the prom night you never had."

* * * * *

The air in the room had cooled considerably as night approached. Neither one of them seemed bothered by the chill as their desire kept them hotter than the inside of a furnace. The sun had disappeared over the horizon, leaving the room draped in darkness. Tanner shut the window and lit the candles on the side table. The warm flickering light silhouetted their bodies.

He took a small step back and perused the naked woman before him. The soft glow of the candlelight made her honey-gold skin glisten. By God, she was exquisite. It wasn't just her physical appearance that attracted him. There was something about her. Something that drew him in and tugged at his emotions. She was unlike any other woman he'd ever been with. In fact, she was everything he'd ever been looking for. How could he not remember her? Ally's voice pulled him back to the situation at hand.

"Let me down from here," she demanded, her eyes flashing with anger and something else. If he had to guess, he'd say passion, anticipation.

He stepped closer, until he could feel the heat radiating from her body. Using the backs of his fingers, he trailed a line down her face. Her skin felt so soft beneath his hand. Looking at her made him wild with the need to fuck her. She stiffened and twisted her head sideways, breaking his touch.

She glared at him and blew out a shaky breath. "The sheriff is outside waiting for me. I could scream." Her voice rose an octave.

He smiled and skated a finger over the milky curve of her breasts. He could feel her heart pounding inside her chest. His fingers dropped to her cunt and threaded through the fine hair between her thighs. He caressed her nether lips and parted her folds. His fingers quickly became drenched with her moisture.

When he wiggled his finger, she arched into him and bit down on her bottom lip. Her action was so telling. She was excited. That pleased him.

"Yes, you could," he said, his voice rough. "If you wanted to," he challenged.

"Of course I want to," she said, her cheeks turning one shade pinker. He watched her throat as she swallowed.

His grin widened as he lightly massaged her engorged clit. "Now why would you do that, Ally? Why would you deny yourself what you really want?"

She opened her mouth and he silenced her with a kiss. He pressed his lips over hers. Hard. Possessively. He traded hot, wet kisses with her for a long, endless moment, until his touch penetrated her defenses. Soon her lips widened and her tongue moved inside to mate with his. Every sensual movement of her body indicated her wants and desires.

He let out a low growl of longing as he began to devour her with his mouth. He pressed his cock against her, letting her know the effect she had on him. When she began whimpering for more, he buried his face in the side of her neck. He lingered there, breathing in her erotic scent.

His cock throbbed painfully, screaming for release. But he wasn't about to give into his need just yet. First he wanted to drive this luscious naked woman beyond the brink of sanity. He wanted to stir the fire in her until she begged for release.

"Please, Tanner, more. I want more." She squirmed and tossed her head to the side. "I want to feel you inside me."

A sound rumbled deep in his throat. "Ah, now it's *you* who begs." Dropping the crop he still clutched in one hand, he quickly discarded his pants and removed his shirt. His hands gripped the side of her hips and held her pelvis close to his. His cock scraped her swollen clit. Her sigh of sweet pleasure filled the room.

He twisted his head and examined the contents on the table beside him. The candlelight flickered across the ceiling, creating shadows and providing him with enough light to examine the sex toys on display.

His blood began racing with anticipation. "What do we have here?" he asked, stepping away to grab the nipple clamps. "Were you planning on using these on me?"

She shook her head as her eyes lit up with apprehension. "No. Those aren't mine."

He turned the clamps over in his hands and smiled at her. Ally's chest began to rise and fall quickly. "Tanner..." Her voice was a hesitant whisper.

"Shhhh." He pressed a finger to her lips.

She swallowed her protests when he bent forward and licked the creamy valley between her heavy breasts. A bead of perspiration trickled down her chest and he leaned in and tracked it with his tongue. Her soft moan of pleasure reached his ears. He took one hard nipple between his lips and grazed his teeth over the delicate flesh. Drawing the rock-hard nub deeper into his mouth, he suckled until hollows pulled at his cheeks. He felt her go wild under his gentle assault. She took deep gulping breaths as he treated her other nipple to the same erotic pleasure. Before she had time to protest further, he attached the nipple clamps to her breasts.

Pitching forward, her eyes opened wide in surprise. She moistened her lips and gasped. By small degrees her expression changed from apprehension to excitement. "Tanner that feels...I don't know. It hurts, but it feels incredible at the same time." He pulled on them just a little and she whimpered.

Tanner grabbed the crop and began dragging it over her quivering flesh. "You've been a naughty girl, Ally. What made you think you could keep me captive and torture me by making me watch you pleasure yourself? Didn't you think there would be consequences?" When she didn't answer he pulled on the nipple clamps. "I asked you a question," he growled.

Her head lolled to the side. "I...I don't know." He watched her lids flicker as her eyes darkened with desire.

Tanner circled around her. Reaching down, he used all his strength to tear the bindings around her lush backside, giving him access to her most intimate areas. He pulled apart her perfectly sculpted, heart-shaped ass cheeks. She clenched her pink puckered hole. He stroked the tender flesh with the tip of his finger and she squirmed. Careful to avoid the web, he put his lips close to her ear and whispered, "Naughty girls must be punished, Ally." He pushed one long finger into her tight opening. Her heat curled around him like a glove.

"Tanner..." she whimpered, her voice merely a breathless whisper.

Something in her voice was so comforting, so familiar. It seeped inside him and filled him with warmth. A rush of feelings exploded through him and left him shaken. He was unprepared for the onslaught. In that instant, he knew what he felt for her was more than just a sexual pull. He also knew how easily it would be to lose himself, heart and soul, in this sweet, sexy, *amazing* woman.

Her head rolled to the side. "Tanner," she whispered again as he worked his finger inside her. God, he loved the way she said his name.

It amazed him how important her pleasure had suddenly become to him, and how deeply they'd connected on an intimate level. Tanner wanted nothing more than to give her a wonderful experience, a "first time" experience that she'd never had with another man.

The sudden image of her with another man filled him with an unexpected rage. What the hell was going on with him? He couldn't explain it—couldn't explain all the muddled feeling and emotions churning inside him. All he knew was he wanted to be her first for a lot of things. Her first *and* her last. If another man touched her, he just might have to kill him.

Chapter Four

ဢ

Ally had never felt anything quite like Tanner's finger probing her ass. It was both pain and pleasure mingled into one. When she wiggled her backside, Tanner growled and pushed his finger in deeper.

"Tell me, Ally. Have you ever been fucked here?" He pulled his finger out, spread her cheeks wider, and rubbed the crop over her swollen opening.

She shook her head and gasped for her next breath when the crop breached her ringed passage.

"Since I supposedly stood you up on prom night and missed being your first here," he reached around and fondled her pussy, "then perhaps I can be your first *here*." He coaxed the crop in another inch.

He grabbed the bottle of lubricant off the table and poured a generous amount into his hand. "How does that sound, Ally? Do you want me to be your first?"

"Tanner, I don't think..." Her words trailed off when he withdrew the crop and his slick finger reentered her ass.

"I'll make it good for you, Ally. I promise," he whispered, easing in deeper.

She cried out and bucked against him. "Oh God, that feels incredible." Arching her back, she granted him deeper access. He worked his finger inside her for a long time, until she got used to the new feeling. She thought she was going to go mad with desire. The barrage of sensations made her body convulse. Suddenly it wasn't enough. She wanted more—*all* of him inside her.

"Please put your cock in me," she begged, ramming her ass harder against his finger. Her pussy dripped with desire.

The scent of her arousal began to permeate the room, bringing her passion to new heights.

She could hear his breathing change and knew he was fighting for control. "No. First you'll fuck the crop until you get used to the feel." Even though he tried to sound harsh, she detected gentleness and caring in his voice. His tone softened. "Then maybe I'll let you have my cock." His words touched something deep inside her and stirred her emotions. She suspected she knew the real reason he didn't give her what she begged for. Taking her comfort and wellbeing into consideration, Tanner knew his impressive thickness would be too much for her bear her first time.

She bit down on her bottom lip and fisted her hands above her head when he slathered her opening with warm lubricant. He eased the long crop inside her. She let out a little gasp as it filled her. Closing her eyes she concentrated on the tiny points of pleasure. Her body began to tremble from the stimulation.

"You're so fucking hot, Ally. My cock is throbbing watching you take the crop into your ass." His voice caressed her flesh.

She had no idea being penetrated this way could be so pleasurable. Tanner seemed to know just what to do and just how to touch her. The sensual hunger he aroused in her was shocking. It was a pure carnal delight. She emitted a deep primal sound from the depths of her throat. She felt the muscles in her cunt begin to quiver.

His breath was hot on her neck. "Are you enjoying this, Ally? Do you like me being the first here?" he tenderly whispered into her ear, concern evident in his tone.

She couldn't find her voice to answer. Her throat was too tight with emotion. Instead, she arched her back, driving the crop in deeper. Tanner's hand slid over her hips and parted her labia. When he feathered his finger over her clit she felt herself explode into a million fragments. Her head thrashed side to side as she tumbled into a powerful orgasm.

He eased the crop out and gently ran a soothing finger over her sensitive tissue. "I think your ass has had enough for today." He circled around her until they were eye to eye. He removed the nipple clamps and tossed them aside. "I didn't hurt you, did I?"

God, the compassion and concern in his eyes warmed her all over.

She shook her head from side to side and tried to recapture her breath. "No. It was perfect," she whispered, surprised that she was able to find her voice.

He reached down and stroked her slick cunt while his gaze settled on her mouth. "You're so wet, Ally. Do you know what that does to me?"

Aching to caress his face, she tugged on the binding strands, hoping to snap them. "It's what you do to me, Tanner. It's never been like this for me before. It's never been this good," she blurted out.

He furrowed his brow, aware of the emotions surging through him. "Why, Ally? Why is it so good with me?"

He watched her eyes turn glossy as she lifted her gaze to his. "Because I love you. I've never stopped loving you, Tanner." Her voice ended on a soft whisper.

He jerked his head back, his jaw dropping open. She lowered her lashes, shadowing her eyes.

Tanner nudged her chin up with his thumb. "It's never been this good for me before either, Ally," he admitted. He gave her a warm smile. "Sex has always just been about physical pleasure to me, but you make me feel something in here." He pressed his hand over his heart then leaned forward and gave her a gentle, tender kiss on her forehead. "I don't know why. Honestly, I don't *know* you well enough to have feelings for you. But I *do* have feelings. Strong feelings." He shook his head. "I can't explain it to you because I barely understand it myself."

There was so much emotion in his voice it took her breath away. Ally felt her heart do a somersault while her stomach did cartwheels. She drew in a shuddery breath and absorbed the heat radiating from his body.

He ran his fingers up her arms until his hands locked with hers. His mouth hovered over her lips. She could feel his cock throb against her body. "Tell me how you like it, baby. Do you like it hard and fast or soft and slow?"

The fire in his eyes began burning her up. "It doesn't matter, Tanner. All that matters is that it's you who is giving it to me."

He grew quiet for a moment and then said, "Do you really love me?" His expression was bewildered, his voice full of disbelief.

A surge of warmth flooded her veins and she had a hard time filling her lungs. "I've never loved anyone but you, Tanner." Her voice trembled. "When you ran away, you took my heart with you."

He cupped her face as his mouth closed over hers for a deep, passionate kiss. She felt his thick cock probe her opening.

"Please, Tanner. Let me down from here. I need to hold you in my arms again, just one more time."

With a quick, forceful tug he tore the silky bindings from her hands and pulled her to him. She collapsed against a wall of packed muscle. Burrowing her face in the crook of his neck, she inhaled his familiar scent while focusing on his touch and the feel of his skin against hers.

He gathered her into his arms and backed her up against the wall. Her body fit against his perfectly. She instinctively wrapped her legs around his back. "Fuck me, Tanner."

"No," he said. His gaze was powerful, unguarded.

She looked at him questioningly. Her brows knitted together as she frowned. "No?" Need made her voice husky.

He trailed a kiss over her jaw and looked at her with pure desire. "No, baby. I'm going to *make love* to you. The way you said we were supposed to years ago." There was such tenderness in his gaze.

Her pulse leapt in her throat. Ally twined her arms around his neck and pulled him closer. Her breasts pressed against his chest. She couldn't seem to get him close enough. She cried out his name as he pushed his thick cock into her. With slow, steady strokes he massaged the tight walls of her pussy, drawing out her pleasure.

"You feel amazing," he murmured into her mouth. His voice covered her like a warm blanket as he filled her with his heat. When she squirmed against him, he pumped harder and faster. She could feel his cock throbbing inside her.

"Tanner...*please*." Her voice quivered as she cried out to him. In her haze of arousal she had no idea what she was begging for. She only knew she needed him to ease the escalating tension building inside her.

She squeezed her cunt muscles around his cock. "Mmmm..." he moaned against her skin.

Reaching between their bodies, he pressed his fingers over her swollen clit, coaxing her body into release. Waves of pleasure began washing over her.

She threw her head back and gasped. "Don't stop," she whimpered as her release approached.

"I don't ever plan on stopping. Not today, not tomorrow, not next week. I'll never stop making love to you, Ally."

His words sent her over the edge. Her pussy began to spasm. She arched against him, drawing his cock deeper inside. She called his name and gasped in pleasure when his fingers caressed her sensitive flesh.

He lowered his head and drew her nipple into his mouth. The feel of his warm lips closing over her breast was exquisite. Her body shook as he laved her tight peak with his tongue. She went wild in his arms. She scraped her nails over his back and came apart completely. She felt Tanner's release shudder through him as he slammed into her and pinned her back to the wall.

He closed his mouth over hers and drew her in for a soul-searching kiss. She remained pressed against him until their hearts and bodies fused into one.

Tanner broke the kiss and finger-combed her hair off her face. He gave her a warm smile. He opened his mouth to say something but then shut it again. He looked perplexed. She looked into his eyes searching for answers but all she saw was unanswered questions.

"What is it?" she asked.

He gave a slight shake of his head. "Nothing." She was astonished by the tenderness in his voice.

Ally suspected she knew what he was thinking. "Why is it you can't remember me? Remember *us*?" Once again, Ally's stomach curdled, wondering if witchcraft was indeed involved. But who would do this to him? To her? And why?

Tanner shook his head sadly. He didn't have an easy answer. "I'm not sure."

"Well, well... What do we have here?"

Chapter Five
❧

Tanner and Ally both spun around at the sound of the voice. When Tanner spotted a shadow in the dark corners of the doorway, he hooked his arm around Ally's waist and positioned her behind him. A moment later a beautiful woman stepped into the room. He vaguely recognized the girl with the long black hair and shimmering sapphire eyes. A knot tightened in his gut as he stared at her. There was something about her eyes. Something hauntingly familiar. Something…hypnotizing.

She stepped closer and slowly walked over to the table that held the used sex toys. The light from the flickering candle cast shadows across her porcelain profile. She twisted around to face them and pouted.

"Seems I'm a little late for the party."

Tanner heard a small gasp escape from Ally. She grabbed him by the shoulder and whispered in his ear. "I need my pants."

He quickly scooped Ally's clothes off the floor and handed them to her. She hurried into her pants and pulled on her T-shirt. Tanner shrugged on his own shirt and climbed into his jeans.

"Do I know you?" he asked, widening his stance as though prepared for battle.

As soon as the girl smiled, it hit him. She was the one who had captured him. The last thing he remembered before Ally had come to his rescue was having a conversation about the Belhaven high-school reunion.

Tanner blinked his eyes and shook his head, trying to remember what had happened before he'd woken up bound to the web. He broke out in a cold, uncomfortable sweat. "What did you do to me?" he growled. He listened with half an ear to Ally's low whispered chant behind him. What in the hell was she doing?

The dark-haired girl emitted a deep, sultry laugh from the depths of her throat. "Well, it seems I didn't get a chance to do *anything* to you. It looks like my lovely cousin got to you first."

Tanner spun around and glared at Ally. "*Cousin*? You were in on this?"

Ally shook her head then glared at the dark-haired witch. "Selina's responsible for this, not me."

Tanner stepped back and shook his head. "Would somebody *please* tell me what's going on here?"

They ignored him and glared at each other.

"Selina, what are you doing? Why are you back in town? And why would you do this to Tanner?" Ally asked, her voice rising with each question.

Selina folded her arms across her chest and grinned. "Now what kind of greeting is that, little cousin?"

"How did you get here?"

Selina's grin widened. "Bad *always* prevails over good, Ally. Haven't you learned that by now? I managed to find a way around your *ancient* banishment spell." She rolled her eyes. "As you know, I had many years to work on it."

Banishment spell. Tanner wrestled with half forgotten memories. They were *witches*?

Ally slipped her hand into the front pocket of her jeans. "What do you want with Tanner?"

Selina's eyes darkened to black coals. Her jaw twitched. "Why do you care? He never loved *you*. If he had, he wouldn't have made love to me on prom night before he deserted you and joined the military."

Tanner watched Ally's shoulders stiffen. She shook her head in disbelief. "You were with me on prom night, Selina," she countered.

"Before that, cousin. While you stood on your porch and waited for Tanner, he was making love to me."

Face red with anger, Ally took a step toward Selina, but Tanner held her back. "He never would have done that," Ally bit out.

"If you don't believe me, ask him yourself."

Ally's mouth twisted as though she'd just sucked on a lemon. "I can't. It seems he's lost all recollection of that night. All recollection of *me* and the love we shared."

Tanner's head bobbed back and forth as he tried to follow the conversation. Tried to put together the pieces of the puzzle.

A mischievous grin curled Selina's lips.

Ally let out a humorless laugh and shook her head in disgust. "I can't believe you're responsible for this. Why, Selina? Why would you delete Tanner's memories? Why would you do this to him? To *me*?" she asked in a low, deceptively calm voice.

Like a bow stretched to the limit, Selina's composure snapped. She took a step forward and reached for something in her pocket. Tanner fisted his hands and waited. He wasn't about to let anything happen to Ally.

"He would have wanted me if *you* hadn't come along. Little Miss Perfect with a sweeter than sugar smile. The little tomboy who grew into a gorgeous cheerleader with all the popular friends. While I sat at home alone with no one."

Ally's eyes softened. "But you had me. And I thought we had each other."

Selina huffed. "We had each *other*? Are you forgetting you banished me to the netherworld?"

"Only for your own good, Selina. What you were doing to the townsfolk was wrong, and you know it. If they had gotten their hands on you before I sent you away, it could have been a lot worse. I was protecting you."

"I didn't need or want your protection, little miss good witch. Didn't you ever think I would tire of being in your *perfect* shadow?" Selina waved her hand through the air and snarled. "But I fixed you, *all* the women of Belhaven who preferred your friendship over mine, and all men who never gave me the time of day. I made everybody in this town *pay* for overlooking me."

Ally stepped forward. "The townsfolk will pay no more for your imagined insults," she assured her.

In a motion so fast it took Tanner off guard, Ally pulled a packet out of her pocket and sprinkled the contents over Selina. Keeping a wide berth, Ally circled her cousin and began chanting a spell.

Selina laughed. "Oh please, little cousin. Your magic has grown weak from lack of use." Reaching into her own pocket, Selina pulled out a vial. "Now it's time for *you* to go visit the netherworld. And *you* won't be coming back." Selina glanced at Tanner. "But don't worry, Ally. I promise to take extra special care of *him*."

Ally twisted around and glanced at Tanner. "Get out of here now, while you still can."

"I'm not going anywhere without you, Ally. Ever again."

A movement at the door drew their attention. Tanner turned and spotted the sheriff.

Selina's eyes widened in delight. "*Sheriff*," she purred. "How nice of you to join us. Don't worry, I have something *extra-special* planned for you. No one turns me down without paying for it."

The sheriff drew his gun. Selina threw her head back and laughed. In that split second, Tanner lunged for her and knocked her off balance.

The vial flew into the air. Before it hit the floor and smashed, Ally grabbed it.

She pulled the rubber stopper free. "Tanner, *move!*"

As soon as Tanner distanced himself, Ally threw the potion on Selina and once again recited the spell.

A thick fog covering her, Selina cried out and lunged for Ally, but before she could grab hold, her body turned translucent. "I'll be back, Ally. Wait and see…"

"Not this time, you won't." Ally brushed her palms together. "You were wrong, dear cousin. Good *always* prevails over evil." She turned to the sheriff.

He scratched his head and gave her a genuine smile. "Thank you, Ally." Taking his notebook from his pocket, he turned. "This place gives me the creeps. I'll meet you both outside." His boots pounded the floor as he hurried outside.

Suddenly, as though he'd been struck by a wrecking ball, Tanner flew backwards and hit the wall. He cracked his head and winced in pain. When he opened his eyes and looked up, Ally was standing over him. Her eyes were full of worry. She knelt down and brushed his hair off his forehead.

"Tanner, are you okay?" Her voice trembled. "Please be okay, my heart couldn't take losing you again."

Tanner looked deep into Ally's eyes as old memories flooded him. "Ally Cat," he said softly and pulled her down onto the floor with him.

Her relief was obvious. "Oh my God, Tanner, you remember." Her voice caught on a sob as tears pooled on her lashes.

He shook his head and smiled. "Your spell must have broken the one Selina had over me." He pulled her into his arms and she molded herself against him. Every forgotten emotion he'd ever had for her filled his heart. His insides ached with the love that overcame him. "I never slept with her, Ally. She tried to lure me into her bed, but I turned her down. That must be why she cast a spell over me and erased you from my memory."

"It's okay, Tanner. I believe you."

He cupped her chin and lifted her face until her eyes met his. "Baby, we've lost so much time together. I'm so sorry this happened."

"I know. Me too." The sadness in her heart was apparent.

He brushed her tears from her cheeks. "I love you, Ally Cat."

She closed her hand over his and sniffed. "I love you too, Tanner," she echoed. "I've never stopped."

He pulled her impossibly closer and she melted against him. "I always felt like there was something missing from my life, and now I know what it is. I want to make love to you every day for the rest of our lives to make up for all the lost time." He tilted his head to kiss her.

She inched her head back and looked at him. "One question." A sudden gleam sparkled in her eyes.

"What is it?" he asked, nuzzling her neck, inhaling her rich female scent.

"When do we start?"

Also by Cathryn Fox

ഇ

Ellora's Cavemen: Seasons of Seduction III (*anthology*)
Liquid Dreams
Unleashed

About the Author

ಜಾ

If you're looking for Cathryn Fox you'd never find her living in Eastern Canada with a husband, two young children and a chocolate Labrador retriever. Nor would you ever find her in a small corner office, writing all day in her pajamas.

Oh no, if you're looking for Cathryn you might find her gracing the Hollywood elite with her presence, sunbathing naked on an exotic beach in Southern France, or mingling with the rich and famous as she sips champagne on a luxury yacht in the Caribbean. Perhaps you can catch her before she slips between the sheets with a man who is as handsome as he is wealthy, a man who promises her the world.

Cathryn Fox is no ordinary woman. Men love her. Women want to be her.

Cathryn is bold, sensuous and sophisticated. And she is my alter ego.

Cathryn welcomes comments from readers. You can find her website and email address on her author bio page at www.ellorascave.com.

Tell Us What You Think

We appreciate hearing reader opinions about our books. You can email us at Comments@EllorasCave.com.

Why an electronic book?

We live in the Information Age—an exciting time in the history of human civilization, in which technology rules supreme and continues to progress in leaps and bounds every minute of every day. For a multitude of reasons, more and more avid literary fans are opting to purchase e-books instead of paper books. The question from those not yet initiated into the world of electronic reading is simply: *Why?*

1. *Price.* An electronic title at Ellora's Cave Publishing and Cerridwen Press runs anywhere from 40% to 75% less than the cover price of the exact same title in paperback format. Why? Basic mathematics and cost. It is less expensive to publish an e-book (no paper and printing, no warehousing and shipping) than it is to publish a paperback, so the savings are passed along to the consumer.

2. *Space.* Running out of room in your house for your books? That is one worry you will never have with electronic books. For a low one-time cost, you can purchase a handheld device specifically designed for e-reading. Many e-readers have large, convenient screens for viewing. Better yet, hundreds of titles can be stored within your new library—on a single microchip. There are a variety of e-readers from different manufacturers. You can also read e-books

on your PC or laptop computer. (Please note that Ellora's Cave does not endorse any specific brands. You can check our websites at www.ellorascave.com or www.cerridwenpress.com for information we make available to new consumers.)

3. *Mobility.* Because your new e-library consists of only a microchip within a small, easily transportable e-reader, your entire cache of books can be taken with you wherever you go.

4. *Personal Viewing Preferences.* Are the words you are currently reading too small? Too large? Too... ANNOYING? Paperback books cannot be modified according to personal preferences, but e-books can.

5. *Instant Gratification.* Is it the middle of the night and all the bookstores near you are closed? Are you tired of waiting days, sometimes weeks, for bookstores to ship the novels you bought? Ellora's Cave Publishing sells instantaneous downloads twenty-four hours a day, seven days a week, every day of the year. Our webstore is never closed. Our e-book delivery system is 100% automated, meaning your order is filled as soon as you pay for it.

Those are a few of the top reasons why electronic books are replacing paperbacks for many avid readers.

As always, Ellora's Cave and Cerridwen Press welcome your questions and comments. We invite you to email us at Comments@ellorascave.com or write to us directly at Ellora's Cave Publishing Inc., 1056 Home Avenue, Akron, OH 44310-3502.

COMING TO A BOOKSTORE NEAR YOU!

ELLORA'S CAVE

Bestselling Authors Tour

UPDATES AVAILABLE AT

WWW.ELLORASCAVE.COM

erridwen, the Celtic Goddess of wisdom, was the muse who brought inspiration to story-tellers and those in the creative arts. Cerridwen Press encompasses the best and most innovative stories in all genres of today's fiction. Visit our site and discover the newest titles by talented authors who still get inspired - much like the ancient storytellers did, once upon a time.

Cerridwen Press

www.cerridwenpress.com

Discover for yourself why readers can't get enough of the multiple award-winning publisher Ellora's Cave.

Whether you prefer e-books or paperbacks,

be sure to visit EC on the web at
www.ellorascave.com

for an erotic reading experience that will leave you breathless.